Escape from Aliya

John Hash

ISBN 978-0-9992755-0-4

1

Escape from Aliya is a work of fiction. Any resemblance of any character to any person, living or dead, is unintended and coincidental.

This book is dedicated to the memory of Sandy, Dick, John, Tim, Terry, Pat, and Larry, who gave their lives so long ago that we might stay free.

Glossary of terms:

ACARS (Aircraft Communication Addressing and Reporting System, Classic and Primary) is an aircraft radio band reporting system between aircraft and ground stations or satellites. It constantly reports aircraft parameters to a ground station. Its transmissions are either Classic, or thorough parameter, or Primary or Aero, which only reports whether the aircraft is on the ground, at the gate, off the ground and enroute.

NSA - The National Security Agency, based at Fort Meade, Maryland. Primary electronic, radio, telephone, voice and text, computer email, and basically any other electronic transmission observer and collector. Major analytic installations at Fort Meade and Fort Huachuca, Arizona. Major storage facility in the remote desert of Utah.

CIA – Central Intelligence Agency. Collector and analyst of intelligence outside the United States.

Poseidon – A modified Boeing 737 fitted with electronics gear and long range fuel tanks and equipped for very high altitude loitering. At loiter speeds, it can stay aloft for twenty hours.

SCIF- Sensitive Compartmented Information Facility. Many upper level government leaders have these at their disposal so they can make policy with their staffs and meet with others in security.

Poseidon – A modified Boeing seven thirty seven aircraft, designated P-8, by the United States Navy, equipped with the latest and most thorough electronics, communications and signals gathering equipment, with long range tanks so it can loiter over an area for many hours, and which carries a crew and complement of twelve.

Buk 1 – Surface to air missile, Russian. SA-11. NATO code name: Gadfly. Proximity fuse, shrapnel. Downed the Maylasian Airliner over Ukraine, Russian controlled.

FAL – A seven decimal six five millimeter automatic rifle, originally designed for Fabrique National of Belgium, by Dieudonne Saive, the protege of John Moses Browning, designer of the Colt Model 1911 and the Browning Hi-Power pistols and the Browning M2 fifty caliber machine gun. The FAL subsequently became the chosen firearm of the troops of fifteen nations. The name, translated from the French Fusil Automatique Leger, means rifle, automatic, light. It is chambered for the NATO round, commonly called .308 Winchester in this country, and has an effective range of six hundred meters.

Vr– Rotation speed for a transport category aircraft.

V-ref – The approach to landing speed of a transport category aircraft, taking its present weight and other factors into account.

V-1 - The minimal take off speed of a transport category aircraft, taking its present weight and other factors into account.

Lockheed L-1011 - A large three engine passenger jet manufactured by Lockheed Aircraft between 1970 and 1984. A total of two hundred forty nine were manufactured. Passenger load was a maximum of four hundred. It had a range of four thousand nautical miles at a departure weight of five hundred ten thousand pounds and a full fuel load of thirty one thousand six hundred forty two gallons.

LORAN - Loran is a long range land or sea based system of broadcast stations on very low frequencies with stations all over the world. It uses triangulation to allow receivers to know their location. The system is completely passive, so the receiver cannot be detected. GPS, on the other hand, is a satellite based system that also uses triangulation to allow receivers to know their locations.

Escape from Aliya

As Lero came into the Quonset hut, it took him a moment or two to adjust his eyes to the subdued light. Dr. Voerward was standing in front of Jean who was sitting in a canvas back chair looking wilted. He looked up and said to Lero, "We need to draw blood to test for the Zika virus. This whole district is infested."

"There is no temporary danger of her spreading the Zika virus. If she bleeds, we will be careful and she will not share bodily fluids with anyone before she is tested. The UN team doctor briefed us. Besides, we need to leave right away. You may not draw blood from her. She is in danger of an embolism in this heat and in her condition. Where is the nearest general hospital?"

"The nearest general hospital is in Mombasa, over a hundred miles from here."

"If you draw blood, how can you test it? There are no laboratories here."

"We will send it to Mombasa on the train tomorrow."

"Why don't we just take her to Mombasa? She seems up to the trip."

"The area is quarantined. She may not leave."

"We have orders to leave immediately. We cannot stay. Rebel forces are closing in on the village. We need to leave now" said Lero.

"I insist you stay," said the Doctor.

Lero had his hand on his pistol and had already applied initial pressure to the double action trigger. Just as he was about to draw it out of his pocket, there was a sound of automatic weapons' fire and the hut was struck by several bullets.

The doctor ducked under a nearby table and Lero grabbed Jean by the wrist and they hustled out the front door. Lero's Land Rover was just outside and they piled into it and were off in a few seconds. As Lero accelerated them southward, he could see large clouds of dust and smoke in the rear view mirror. The road was too bumpy for much speed, but he managed forty five miles per hour for several minutes. Once they reached the paved road, he accelerated substantially and they sped for Mombasa.

Jean asked, "How did you find me so fast?"

"Bumbi knew where you were going. Just lucky I got there when I did. I hope he and his family escape harm. Those rebels are killing everyone in their path. If the government troops don't respond quickly, there will be a blood bath."

"Why are we leaving, anyway? We were just getting settled in."

"Mr. Murfree needs our help with something. He said there would be a plane waiting for us at the airstrip at the missionary base down the road about ten miles. He said to just leave the Land Rover and hide the key under the right front tire. They will retrieve it later."

By the time he finished telling her that, they could see the airstrip ahead, parallel to the road. There was a Cessna Caravan sitting at the north end of the runway with the propeller turning. Lero turned into the entrance and brought them parallel to the Caravan about fifty yards off of the dirt runway. They got out and he hid the key and they walked quickly to the plane, with Lero holding onto Jean's arm. Carlos opened the door for them when he saw them get within a few yards of the plane. They wasted no time getting on board and leaped into seats across the aisle from each other. Before they could bounce once, the pilot came in with throttle and they were accelerating down the strip. Dust flew up around and behind the plane as it accelerated and in a few seconds, they were airborne. Lero could tell that the pilot left full throttle in as he leveled them off at five thousand feet. He grabbed a head set from the hook on the side of the cabin.

Carlos saw him do that and immediately asked, "Are you guys okay? Any problems?"

"Jean is running a fever and feels kinda dumpy, but other than that, we are good to go."

"Good doctors at the alternate base, but we will not have time for her to be examined."

"Not going to Mombasa?" asked Lero.

"Negative. Jet is waiting for you at alternate."

"Okay, thanks," answered Lero and the conversation ceased.

In a few minutes, Carlos said, "Field in sight. You all need to go directly to the jet, please."

"Must be something hot," said Lero.

"I think so. You guys be careful," said Carlos.

"Thanks for coming to get us, Carlos. Don't know when we will get a chance to properly thank you."

"Don't worry about that. I will just feel a lot better for your safety when I see that jet raise its landing gear. We can meet for Christmas or something."

"Thanks again," said Lero.

Carlos did not call on the radio and since the field was aligned with them pretty well, he just made a straight in approach. The turf runway was smooth and the grass helped decelerate the Caravan. Carlos brought them alongside the Grumman about thirty yards away. Lero was at the door by the time they got stopped and helped Jean down the stairs. They hurried to the jet and Lero waved to Carlos as he pulled up the stairway and closed the door. The pilot had the off side engine running and as they climbed aboard, he started the on-side engine. In twenty seconds, the engine gauges indicated all okay, so he pushed the throttles up and the jet leaped down the runway. The sun was just setting as they climbed northwest.

Lero reached across the aisle and took Jean's hand. He held on as she drifted off to sleep. She was so beautiful as she slept, he thought. Soon, his fatigue caught up to him and he, too, drifted off.

Chapter 2

The change in engine power awakened Lero. His days as an Air Force and commercial pilot made him sensitive to such things. He stretched and looked over at Jean. He eyes were just opening. He got up and crossed over to her seat and kissed her cheek.

"Looks like we are approaching to land," he said.

"Where are we?" she asked, sleepily.

"I don't know. I fell asleep right after you," he said.

Since it was dark out, they could not see much as they plane approached to land. Lero felt the gear come out and lock and shortly after the flaps went down, the G-4 touched down softly and rolled out. The plane taxied up to a squat red brick building with no outward clues as to location. Lero and Jean and the pilots got out and walked stiffly to the building, stretching long unused muscles in the process.

As they entered the reception room, the man at the far side of the room, turned and spoke.

"Glad you are here. Let me get you some food and drink." It was Jefe.

"Jefe, so glad to see you."

Lero and Jean hugged their old friend.

"To answer your questioning looks, Mr. Murfree asked me to meet you and brief you. Alita and I were just returning from Keros on a scheduled stop here in the Canaries when he called and asked me to stay over and meet with you."

"Where is Alita? We would love to see her," said Jean.

"She is waiting in the restaurant. Let's go," said Jefe. "I have a car."

"No luggage?" asked Jefe.

"No luggage," said Lero. "We left in a hurry."

"No problem. Let's go," said Jefe.

Chapter 3

Before you wade into this adventure, you need to be made familiar with the leading characters.

You have walked into an episode in the lives of a group of people you have not met before.

About two years ago, Lero (his nom de guerre) was assigned to a special unit at Davis Monthan Air Force Base in Tucson, Arizona, as a contractor and met Jean there at a church bible study meeting.

Physically, Lero is five feet eleven, weighs one eighty, black hair with some gray in the sideburns, brown eyes. Lero is a former airline pilot who took early retirement when his airline failed ten years ago. Since then, he had been rebuilding jet engines for a large airline based in Western Pennsylvania. Lero had been a widower for three years and Jean had been single for several years after a short marriage in her twenties. She is an avionics technician and a college graduate. She came to Tucson with her father and worked for him in his avionics shop until he retired. He died four years ago. She became a member of Jefe's unit when she reconditioned the radios in the Vulcan bomber that was used in the strike on the underground centrifuge enrichment facility near

Natanz, Iran, that is chronicled in the earlier book, "Lero's Mission." Since then, she has headed the electronic intelligence laboratory and shop for the unit. It was she who designed and built the scanner that intercepted the transmissions regarding the visit of the Grand Ayatollah to Bushehr that enable the team to "paint" his vehicle so the Mirage fighter could hit it. Jean accompanied Lero on the last mission into Disneyland, using the cover that she was his Algerian mistress, while he pretended to be a French avionics technician. Lero was badly hurt when the explosion tore off the front of the hotel from which he was "painting" the target vehicle. Jean and Jefe succeeded in getting an air ambulance into the Bushehr airport to evacuate Lero.

Lero and Jean were both the kind of people who are content to spend time alone, but when they met each other, after years of being alone, they were strongly drawn to each other. As this episode takes place, they have lived together for about two years.

They both worked for Jefe who ran a special unit of contractors at Davis Monthan Air Force Base in Tucson, Arizona. Jefe reported directly to President Thompson, whose nom de guerre is "Mr. Murfree."

(Lero's traveling cover name is Dan Roman. For those inclined to remember aviation trivia, Dan Roman was the co-pilot in the movie "The High and Mighty," played by John Wayne. Lero's "nom de guerre" which each operator has, was chosen by him at the beginning of his first "operation." It is the last syllable of the word "pistolero" which he chose because his hobby is building and shooting target pistols. Only people who are "associated" would know that.)

NOTE: If you have not read "Module Eighteen," an earlier adventure for Lero and Jean and their friends, you need to know about Ernie, too. Ernie's dossier shows that his full name is Ernest Everette Galvin. Born in Lynchburg, Virginia, 1955. Bachelors at the Naval Academy, 1977. Tour of duty on a destroyer in the Mediterranean. Masters in Physics at Duke, 1982. Ph.D. in Nuclear Physics from Princeton, 1986. Resumed Naval Career, promoted through the ranks to Admiral in 1996. Had a disabling stroke in 2006 and retired from active duty. Hired as Physics Professor, University of Arizona, 2007. Married to Joanne for forty one years, grown children and teenaged grandchildren. Research director for the University of Arizona in the Physics Department. Top security clearance. The pictures show an alert, focused man with a high forehead, thinning blonde hair and piercing blue eyes.

Now you need to know some about Jean. Jean is five feet four and weighs one hundred twenty pounds. Her hair is light brown and she has blue eyes.

Lero met Jean during his first mission. Jean was an avionics technician who did contract work for Jefe and earned her place in the unit because of her ability to build and sometimes invent the technical electronics gear that the unit needed for its clandestine operations. She lives adjacent to Davis Monthan Air Base in Tucson. She and Lero met at a Wednesday bible study group at her church. After a couple of meetings, she invited him to dinner. They have lived together for about two years now and are completely devoted to each other.

Jefe was the head of Group 47, which the members usually refer to as the "Unit." The headquarters of the unit is on the air base in a Quonset hut which was erected in the build-up to World War II, but has survived the heat and sunlight of the western desert. It is up-fitted inside now with air conditioning and all the comforts and amenities of a modern office building, even though its dusty exterior is pretty much as it was years ago.

Jefe is sixty four and has recently begun his retirement. President Thompson, to whom the Unit reports directly, asked Lero to take over the Unit when Jefe began his retirement.

Jefe lives with Alita, whom he has known since high school. Alita is married to George, who is in a nursing home in Tennessee after suffering a debilitating stroke several years ago. Alita's children know Jefe as a long-time family friend, but they do not know that Jefe and Alita live together. Her cell phone still carries a 423 area code, so when she visits with her daughters, wherever she is, they think they are talking to her in eastern Tennessee. She keeps a small apartment near the nursing home, but is rarely there. From time to time, Alita must travel to Tennessee to see to George's care and to visit with their daughters, who live about a hundred miles from the nursing home, in different cities.

Jefe and Alita alternate between their home in Tucson and his villa on Keros in the Greek Isles.

You can catch up with the group by reading "Lero's Mission," "Go Get Nadja," "Flight to Oblivion," "Falcon Strike," "Lero Six," "Module 18," and "Grid Strike," by this same author.

Welcome to the unit.

Chapter 4

As they got in the car, Lero asked, "By the way, where are we?"

"We are in the Canary Islands. Your jet crew will refuel the plane and get a meal and be ready to take you onward in a couple of hours."

Then while they drove toward the main terminal building and its nice cafeteria, he explained, "We were sorry to drag you out of Africa so suddenly, but the CIA Director's plane has disappeared under mysterious circumstances. Worse than that, even, his Director of Operations and Director of Clandestine Services were on the plane with him."

"Wow," said Jean and Lero simultaneously.

"Because Mr. Murfree is suspicious that there is a highly placed mole in the CIA, he has asked me to come back into service and work with you, outside the Agency, to see what we can find out and perhaps act on a plan later."

Lero said, "Jean may need some medical attention, Jefe. She is running a fever. Can we get her to a clinic before we leave?"

"Sure. Our British friends maintain a base here. I will call and make arrangements. Would you rather do that first rather than eat first?"

"Yes," they both said, again simultaneously.

Jefe pulled over to the curb of the access road and got out his cell phone.

"Hello, this is Jefe. Commander Robards said I could call if I had need of services."

"Yes, we have a female associate who is running a fever and feeling unwell. May we bring her presently?"

"Thank you. We are enroute. Be there in a few minutes."

Because of their concern for Jean, neither man mentioned eating before they got her to the clinic.

Jefe pulled the Plymouth up to the main gate of the British Forces Base. As the guard leaned over to ask his identity and business, Jefe replied: "I am Harry Brubaker, an American National. I am attached to Unit 47 of the United States Department of Defense. I called earlier to have a female associate examined at your Medical Clinic. Also with me are Dan Roman and Jean Hammond of our unit."

"Wait a minute, sir," said the guard and retreated to his booth while his back-up kept eyes on them all.

In a moment, he returned and said, "The medical clinic is on the right just past the second stop sigh. Each of you should wear these badges identifying you as guests. Thank you, sir."

He stepped back and gave a jaunty salute and waved them forward.

In a few moments, they pulled up in front of the Clinic. Lero kept an attentive grip on Jean's arm as they walked in.

The desk sergeant, Valerie Dunston, rose to speak to them as they approached.

"I am Harry Brubaker. This is Miss Jean Hammond of our unit. We called earlier to request a medical exam for her."

"Yes, Mr. Brubaker, we have been expecting you. Dr. Royster will see her in Exam Room three down the hall to the right."

Lero took Jean to Exam Room Three while Jefe took a seat in the waiting area.

In a few moments, a fiftyish man about five ten and one hundred eighty pounds walked in. He had a stethoscope behind his neck and was dressed in a green scrub uniform.

"I am Doctor Royster. How can I help you?"

Jean spoke first, "Thank you, Doctor. I am Jean Hammond, attached to Unit 47 of the United States Department of Defense. We have been posted to Kenya for about two months and just this afternoon left hurriedly to return to the States under orders. I have been running a fever for a couple of days now and I feel that my condition is deteriorating slowly. This gentleman is my companion Dan Roman. You may converse with him or me about my condition without reservation."

"Okay, let's get a quick blood pressure and pulse."

He finished that quickly and said, "One fifteen over seventy five. Good pressure. Pulse is 68, also good. Let's have a look at your throat."

"Hmmm. He mumbled. You have a very red throat. Have you been taking your Atabrine for malaria?"

"Yes, we took it regularly as prescribed."

"Do you have any history of serious communicable disease, like tuberculosis or measles or chicken pox?"

"No tuberculosis, but I had measles and chicken pox as an adolescent," she said.

'Africa is vast and full of disease," he said. "You may have picked up a germ or two from the water. Even if you did not drink the water, it is hard to avoid contact sometimes. If people cough upwind of you, you could inhale something. I think you have a sore throat without complications. I will give you some Ampicillin to start your treatment. I understand you will be on your way soon. I see no reason to quarantine you, but you should be careful if you need to cough or sneeze near others. Also, we should draw blood to test you and we can report the results through your chain of command. I understand that you are anticipating immediate departure from our area. I recommend that you see a medical doctor when you can after you get stateside. Any questions?"

"No, doctor. Thank you very much."

A nurse stepped in to draw blood and Lero and Jefe left the room to wait on Jean. In a couple of minutes, Jean and the nurse came out of the room. Jean walked to them and the three of them walked back out toward the front door they had entered just a few minutes previously.

After a stop at the water fountain, with a bottle of pills in hand, Jean led the others out of the clinic and back to the car.

Chapter 5

"Do you feel well enough to fly transatlantic tonight," asked Lero of Jean.

"I am alright. The fever is the worst of it. I am clear headed, but have a headache and body aches. I can sleep on the plane. I would rather wake in the U.S. than anyplace else."

"Okay, then," said Jefe. "We will go."

Jefe brought them back to the airport to the fixed base operator. A Customs agent was there and took their identities and credentials and went to telephone his supervisor. In a few minutes, he returned and said they were cleared to leave the Canary Islands. Jefe thanked the officer and they walked out to the plane to talk to the pilots.

Alton McGee and Bart Higgins were waiting near the door of the plane. Jefe and Lero helped Jean on board and then turned to talk with the pilots.

"We need to go as soon as you can leave," said Jefe.

"We are ready to go, sir," said Alton. "We have some food and drinks for you all, so you need not go back for chow."

"Very thoughtful, Alton," said Jefe. "We are good to go then."

Jefe told Jean and Lero about the food and drinks and Lero went aft to the galley to bring them some dinner. Meanwhile, McGee and Higgins activated their flight plan and made ready to start engines.

"Tenerife South Ground, Grumman November 5606 Romeo, at the Fixed Base operator, with Information India, ready in five minutes to taxi to the active for departure to Andrews Joint Base, GPS direct."

November 5606 Romeo, roger. Open flight plan with Tower and report back ready to taxi."

"November 5606 Romeo, Roger, over to tower."

"Tenerife South Tower, November 5606 Romeo, ready to taxi and open flight plan to Andrews Joint Base, GPS direct, with India."

"Roger, November 5606 Romeo, Flight plan approved as filed. Expect two zero, twenty thousand ten after departure. Departure on 126.65. Squawk 3445 for us, please. Runway seven is the active. Pressure two niner, niner seven. Ground when ready to taxi."

"Roger, tower, 5606 Romeo back to ground."

As McGee dealt with the ground and tower transmissions, Higgins started the engines and went through the pre-take off check list with him.

As soon as the gauges indicated all was well, they called ground and got permission to taxi to Runway seven.

As Lero and Jean and Jefe strapped in, the pilots applied take off power and the Grumman G-4 surged down the runway. As soon as they were turned to a heading of two eight five, Jefe and Lero and Jean began to give attention to their meals. They had not eaten in eighteen hours, so they were eager. As they munched, the darkness outside the windows enveloped them all.

After dinner, they did not have any trouble falling asleep. The G-4 bore on through the night at flight level three four zero. It was pitch black.

Chapter 6

The soft chime above them awakened Jefe, Jean and Lero. In a minute, McGee came on the PA and said, "We will be landing at Andrews in about thirty minutes."

Allowing Jean to go first, the each visited the lavatory and stretched and walked around a bit. Lero found some fresh fruit and orange juice cans in the refrigerator and brought them out.

The sun was streaking in the windows and it was a beautiful clear day off the Atlantic Coast. They watched as the coast slid by beneath them and soon thereafter they noticed that the pilots pulled some power off for the descent.

Lero noticed Norfolk Naval Air Station and Langley Air Force Base as they passed over. Then they were over the Chesapeake Bay.

Air Traffic Control brought them in on a right base to Runway three six left at Andrews and they touched down at exactly eight thirty, eastern time.

They taxied up to the smaller terminal and the pilots shut down. Lero and Jean and Jefe thanked the pilots as they came aft to deplane with them.

They were all a bit stiff and walked with effort across the tarmac. Inside the terminal, McGee and Higgins told them that this was as far as they were to go and excused themselves. Again, thanks were offered.

Jefe stepped over to the airman at the counter. Actually, it was Airman Jennifer Radford who greeted him.

"Harry Brubaker and party. We need transportation. Any messages for us?"

"Yes, Mr. Brubaker. Welcome back to the United States and Andrews Joint Base. Your drivers are waiting for you at that dark blue Denali in the parking lot out that east door. They have your destination and will provide transport."

"Thank you, Airman. Have a nice day."

"You, too, Sir," she said.

Jefe returned to Lero and Jean who had visited the rest rooms and were ready to leave.

"I need to visit the restroom, too, and then we will go," Jefe said.

Chapter 7

When he came out they went to the blue Denali to meet their drivers.

"Mr. Brubaker, welcome back," said the driver Carmichael.

"Good to see you again, Steve. Meet Lero and Jean."

Everyone smile and nodded and they got in the Denali.

They left Andrews and got onto the I-495 beltway. About ten miles north, they turned off and approached a two story red brick building set back from the road a bit. The sign in the lawn said, Turner Electronics.

The parking lot was full of vehicles and they walked in. Carmichael and his helper stayed back as they entered the reception room.

Jefe approached the receptionist.

"Harry Brubaker and party, reporting in."

"Good Morning, Mr. Brubaker. You are to meet in Conference room seven down the hall to the right."

When they left the well-lit hallway and stepped into the subdued conference room, it did not take them a second to realize that the man waiting for them was President Thompson.

He warmly greeted them all. It had been several months since they had seen each other and more than a year since all four of them had been together. President Thompson asked each of them in turn to tell him how they were and to voice any concerns.

Jean said that she was running a fever and feeling fatigued. Lero said he was fine, but a bit tired. Jefe the same.

"I want you all to know how much Janice and I appreciate each of you. You are our closest friends in this business and we pray for your safety constantly. Without you all, we would not be able to accomplish so many things that using the government bureaucracies would slow down or prevent. This business with the Director's plane missing is still a mystery. The plane departed Narita at twenty two hundred thirty hours local time on Wednesday. That would have been nine thirty AM here in D.C. The plane reported normally for about three hours, then the radio went silent. The ACARS reporting ceased with the report made about twenty minutes before the other radios went silent. That would have placed the aircraft about fifteen hundred miles east of Tokyo, well out into the Pacific.

Because we wanted to keep it quiet, we sent the Navy patrol aircraft to the area and they have scoured that sector of the ocean with no sightings. Based on some other strange happenings related to the CIA, we suspect that we have a highly placed mole in the Agency or somewhere high up in the government. Soon, we are going to have to announce the disappearance. I intend to let the deputy directors of Clandestine Services and Operations take over for now, but I intend to bring in an outsider to temporarily replace the Director."

He paused to let that information soak in. No one spoke for a minute.

Then he said, "I want you, Jefe, to take over as temporary director." Again he paused to let them react. There were non-verbal expressions of surprise and then Jefe spoke, "Mr. President, Fred, I am deeply honored. This is quite a surprise. When do you want me to start?"

"I want you all to get a good day's rest, and I want you, Harry, to meet me at Langley at two o'clock today for a three o'clock announcement in the auditorium. Dan and Jean, I have need of your services, too, but I want to keep you out of the bureaucracy where you can move without observation. I want all three of you to come for dinner with Janice and me tonight at seven. We can talk business after a nice visit. I want all three of you to buy trac phones today at different vendors. Give the phone numbers to me and only me and share the numbers with each other. I know you all came out on short notice and have no luggage. Use these credit cards to get yourselves clothes and gear and whatever else you need. I need to go now to make the announcement of the disappearance. If you need to contact me before this afternoon and this evening, use the names Robert and Eunice Sprouse if you call the White House. We don't know where this mole is. He or she may even be in the White House. Be careful, as I know you will. Thank you all so much for helping me. I love you guys."

There wasn't much time for a visit, because the President rose and walked out without much more to say.

Jean and Lero and Jefe were left alone in the conference room.

After a pause, they sat at the conference table once again.

Jefe said, "This just goes to show you that you never know, in this business, when the call will come. Alita must be wondering where I am and what I am doing. I need to get her here from Tenerife. Where shall we stay tonight?"

"How about the Marriott at Dulles Airport? It is well out of town, with a lot of international travelers in and out. We would not stick out at all," suggested Lero.

"Good idea. Alita and I stayed there before. I will get us a private car and we can go get some clothes and stuff. We can rent you a car later and get our trac phones."

"First, Jean, let's get you to a doctor, said Lero.

They went out to the rental car that had been made available as Jefe's temporary transport.

"Where is the best place to take Jean?" asked Lero.

Let's go to the University of Maryland at College Park. I know some people there and she can get a world class exam and medical advice," said Jefe.

After a twenty minute drive, filled with questions and answers between them, they arrived at College Park. The Emergency Department entrance was clearly visible and they pulled the car up close in the parking lot.

As they walked in, Jefe went to the desk nurse and said, "I am Harry Brubaker. A lady associate of mine is ill and needs an exam. She is running a fever and feels light headed. Doctor Rangit told me to use his name if I ever needed medical attention here."

"Yes, Mr. Brubaker. Have a seat and I will alert triage. We will call for you on the public address system."

"Thank you," said Jefe.

In less than a minute, the PA system announced, "Patient Brubaker, report to Triage Room Three."

 Jefe led Lero and Jean down the hall to the room.

The duty nurse took Jean's blood pressure and temperature and began her interrogation to narrow the extent of her condition.

After several questions, she said, "I will send you to Dr. Kendall in Exam Room thirteen down the hall. Hope everything works out okay."

"Thank you, Nurse," said Lero for the group.

Once in Room Thirteen, Lero and Jefe waited until the Doctor arrived and until they had answered his questions of them, then they left so Jean and Doctor could complete her examination.

Chapter 8

In the waiting room, Jefe and Lero had a brief opportunity to converse, in low tones, of course.

"This certainly is a fine kettle of fish," said Lero. "I sure hope Jean does not have anything serious."

"Me too," said Jefe. "She will get the best of care here, you can be sure."

"What do you make of the Director's disappearance?" asked Lero.

"The Director back in Bill Casey's day used a C-141, but after that, they downsized and began using a Boeing 757, so it would not stick out so much at civilian airports. I would imagine that it carried the latest in avionics gear, including ACARS. It looks to me like sabotage, maybe a bomb aboard. There is always the possibility of a shoot down at sea by Russia or even North Korea, in that area, too. I will let you know what the guys at the Agency think," Jefe said.

"ACARS got insubstantial coverage when MH370 disappeared two years ago. Based on how long the plane was reporting, it was about fifteen hundred miles east of Japan, so it was reporting directly to the nearest satellite," said Lero.

"I will ask for a briefing from the Defense Intelligence Agency as soon as I am announced by President Thompson. I want to get the viewpoint of an agency outside of the CIA. We are going to have to be very careful with communications from now on. All eyes and ears will be on me for valid and nefarious reasons. Touchy stuff will need to be face to face."

"I understand," said Lero. Jean nodded.

In a few minutes, Dr. Shackelford and Jean came out.

"I think she has a mild case of Dengue Fever. Not unusual for someone on recent arrival from a civilized culture to Africa. We will give her antibiotics to take for a week and it should clear up. I told her to report any change or increase in fever. The blood test results will be available in an hour or so. If you will give a phone number to the duty nurse, we will call you with results. If something unusual appears, we may need to see you again, Ms. Hammond. Any questions?"

"No, Doctor Shackelford. Thank you for seeing me on such short notice," said Jean. She appeared relieved that her malady was no more serious than preliminarily diagnosed.

Dr. Shackelford shook hands with them all and wished them a good day.

Once more in the car, they headed for Dulles Airport around the beltway. Lero and Jean took a room and Jefe did likewise. Once they had keys, they got back in the car and Jefe took them to a car rental agency.

After Lero had rented a new Ford, the three of them got in and had a talk.

"I would expect that I will be tied up with matters for a day or two. Let's go to a mall and get some trac phones and clothes and supplies and then I need to get to Langley. Wow, this is a big day. I wonder how Alita will take this news."

"We are so proud of you, Jefe," said Jean. Lero nodded his agreement. "Let us know when Alita is coming in and we will pick her up and bring her to your motel room."

"I would imagine that it will be relatively safe to converse by trac phone today, since only we and Fred know who will be announced as temporary Director later. I will call you to let you know when Alita is arriving. Thanks for being there for me and her. We are into something big here. I know I will need your help," said Jefe.

Out they went to get their trac phones. Jefe took them to an upscale mall where he went into the Brooks Brothers store and bought three suits and shirts, ties, underwear, socks and cuff links. The sales people were delighted. He asked for immediate tailoring and was told he needed to wait about forty minutes for the trousers and suit coat to be altered. Jefe was delighted with the speedy service.

Lero took Jean, carefully, to an Ann Taylor outlet and got her some outfits, undergarments, hose and other paraphernalia, enough to hold her for a few days until they could do some more leisurely shopping, then he sat her down inside a Joseph A. Bank men's store and went in to get his clothing and gear. By the time they got back to the car, they had also visited the drug store to get tooth brushes, combs, and such supplies, too. Lero snagged a cart for all the bags they had as they left the mall.

After another brief chat, Lero and Jean took their car and went back to the Marriott. Jefe headed for Langley.

Chapter 9

Members of the new media and CIA employees crowded the auditorium. Without an introduction, the President walked out from behind the curtains and approached the podium.

"Ladies and Gentlemen, good afternoon. I need to share some bad news with you. Director Schmidt's aircraft has disappeared over the Pacific about fifteen hundred miles east of Japan. He and Director of Clandestine Services Morgan and Director of Operations, Filbert, and several of their aides were on board. The last report from the aircraft's ACARS reporting system indicated all systems were operating normally. There was no distress call. I have asked the U. S. Navy to search the area near and east of the last reporting location, but they have found nothing so far.

In order to maintain proper function here at the Agency, I have asked the Assistant Director of Clandestine Services and the Assistant Director of Operations to assume those Directorships temporarily.

Because of the special nature of the Director's office and the need to have unfettered communication with the Director, I have decided to choose Harry Brubaker to serve as Acting Director of the Central Intelligence Agency pending more news about the disappearance and hopefully the reappearance of Director Schmidt and his party.

Harry Brubaker has a long a distinguished record of service to the country in the military and in the intelligence community. He may be relatively unknown to the public at large and that is a tribute both to the efforts of the intelligence community to keep the identity of its members closely held, but to Mr. Brubaker's discreet behind the scenes efforts on behalf of the country for more than thirty years.

I want Mr. Brubaker to come out now so you can all get a look at him and take his picture with me for your news outlets. Neither he nor I will make a further statement at this time about the disappearance of Director Schmidt's plane, but we will keep you informed as we receive further reports. Thank you very much."

With that, Jefe stepped out from the curtains and approached President Thompson. They stood for photos for a few minutes, then left by the same way they had entered. Members of the media scurried out to make their reports and upload pictures of Temporary Acting Director Brubaker and the President.

Chapter 10

"You won't believe what has happened," Jefe said to Alita, once he got her on the phone.

"Oh, I don't know," she said. "My lover boy goes running off in the middle of the night and the next thing I know, he is in the U.S. and the President has appointed him Acting Director of the CIA. Just an average day for us."

"How did you know?" he asked.

"The miracle of television. I am so proud of you and so glad President Thompson asked you to serve. Now, how am I going to get out of here and where do I come?" she asked.

"I will arrange a ticket for you, and call you back to give you the airline and the time. Thank you for being so understanding. Lero and Jean will pick you up and take you to our temporary quarters."

"I am so proud of you, Harry. I know the President is relieved to have you in place at such a difficult time."

"You are so sweet to me," he said. "I will call you back as soon as I arrange your ticket. Do you need anything else?"

"No, I am fine. Can hardly wait to see you," she said.

"Me, too. Bye."

"Bye."

Chapter 11

"Can you meet me at the mall where we bought clothes yesterday?" asked Jefe.

"Sure," said Lero. "When?"

"How about four?"

"Okay, see you then." The line went silent.

As Lero drove his Ford into the parking lot of the mall, he spotted Jefe's rental Dodge near a hedge that divided the parking area. As he approached, Jefe saw him and got out of his car and waited beside it for Lero to pull up. He got in the passenger side and said, "Let's go somewhere else to talk. I want to keep you off the grid for as long as I can. I am sure my car is bugged and we may be followed."

Lero wasted no time getting them out of the lot and he blended onto the beltway and accelerated into the left lane. After about five minutes at eighty miles per hour, they were confident that they were not followed, at least by surface means, anyway.

The took the next exit and pulled into a crowded Wendy's parking lot.

Once settled, Lero asked, "Do you want to get something to eat or drink?"

"Let's just talk first," said Jefe.

After a deep breath, he started, "Well, the CIA does not know too much. The search operation is being run by the military and they are reporting directly first to the President and he is letting them update the Agency with what he approves. Still no sightings. The records at ACARS are being examined by experts, but they only show a sudden cessation of normal outputs."

Lero nodded to indicate receipt of the information.

"It probably has nothing to do with Schmidt's disappearance, but there is something else afoot that I need you to get involved in. This is most quiet. The Acting Director of Clandestine Services brought me up to date on this. The President and the now missing Director of the CIA were putting together a plan to fly a large aircraft into an airport in Syria and evacuate a large number of people whose identities as workers for western governments are probably about to be exposed. The Director and the President have talked about this, just the two of them, in the Rose Garden. There are not records or any kind of involvement of the CIA in this as far as we can tell. Compartmentalization made this just an "Eyes Only" project and the President believes that Director Schmidt had not revealed any of this to his people. They intended to put the plan into motion in the future, but had now decided to act. Now, President Thompson wants us to carry out the plan, totally in the black, involving no CIA or other government people. There are agency people, military spec ops people, ours and other country's people, notably IDF, opposition politicians, Christian refugees and others who need extraction. The idea is to use a bogus clearance from a high Syrian official, known only to the President, to let the plane land at night on an airport away from the really hot areas. The refugees, hiding out nearby, will be waiting and will board the plane immediately and it will take off as soon as they board. The plane will get out of Syrian airspace as quickly as possible. The where and when and other logistical details are yet to be worked out. I want you and Jean to head the effort, reporting directly to me so we can keep Fred out of the loop. We don't know now if the mole is in the White House, the CIA, or one of the other intelligence agencies. This is really spooky."

"Wow, Jefe, this is a big order. It reminds me of the Entebbe raid. Do you have a briefing book or something so I can read up and Jean can do the same?"

"Yes. I never told you before, but I was in on the planning for the Entebbe raid. I was in Naval

Intelligence at the time. They detached me to the IDF (Israel Defense Forces) to assist General Dayan any way we could. I ended up in a C-130 gun ship orbiting off the African coast that night. We were to go in and mop up if the situation went south. Fortunately, the Israelis pulled it off smoothly and we did not have to get involved. Enough information to give you what you need now is on this thumb drive. You and Jean are not to allow this to be placed on a computer that is connected to the internet. I know you and she know how to handle this. Let me know when you have things basically arranged. My belief is that choice of the airport or airports is the biggest part of the decision. Your contact is Tarek El Sheeb, a Syrian national, who works for a front organization called Food For Refugees. He is in New York. Here is his address. Best you just walk in to their offices and have all initial contact with him direct and in person. I will supply you with a password that only you and he will know, so you and he can be sure you are talking to the right person. Be careful you are not followed to New York. You and he can decide how to communicate thereafter. Now, you better take me back to my car. I need to get back. By the way, my trac phone number is 703 455-8822."

Lero wrote it down and then said, "Okay. Thanks, I think, for involving me and Jean in this. We will give you our best effort."

"I know you will, Dan. Thanks."

Chapter 12

When Lero got back to the room at the Marriott, after a hug and a smooch, but before he explained to Jean what Jefe had said, even though they were very confident that the room was not yet bugged, he turned up the TV nice and loud and held her close while he whispered in her ear what Jefe had told him.

When he finished, they turned the TV down and resumed "normal" conversation.

Jean said, "If we are going to be here for a while, I need a laptop and you need one, too. Let's get lunch and go shop for them."

"Okay," he said, and they started for the car.

"As much progress as they have made with lap tops, we can get one that is nicely sized to fit in my handbag. You might want one, too." she said.

"I just need something big enough to be able to type without too much difficulty," he said.

In a few minutes down the road, they spotted an upscale mall and entered. They bought trac phones separately, her first. He waited a few minutes after she bought hers and then walked over to another kiosk to get his.

"I think it best that we not put often called numbers into these phones. You need to memorize mine and Jefe's number. He showed her the slip of paper with Jefe's number,703 455-8822. Then he showed her the tag on his trac phone which read 703 455-8989. What is yours?" he asked.

Jean opened her trac phone box and showed him the number. Even as early in the game as this was, she was using the best tradecraft, not speaking the number out loud. 703 455-9123.

"I see they have a Japanese walk up restaurant at the food court. Would you like some sweet and sour chicken and rice?" he asked.

"Sure, it will help me calm the pit of my stomach. It has that 'Here we go again' feeling.

As they ate, he told her he thought it best that they go back to the room, after they bought any other supplies they needed, to unpack her laptop and his and review the contents of the thumb drive.

She gave him that doe-in-the-headlights look and said, "I still have not gotten all the aches out of my shoulders from sleeping on the plane. I am going to get in a nice steamy shower and soak for a while after we get back. I noticed that the showers have a nice bench in them. Maybe you could let me sit on your lap while I soak."

Lero experienced that familiar tug in his belly when she said that. He swallowed and said, "Sure. It would be my pleasure."

He waited while she found a computer store and bought her laptop. Then she returned and told him the model she had bought and he went to the same store and bought a similar model. She told him she used the female salesperson in the blue outfit, so he picked one of the guys to buy his from. He walked back to the food court and then together they walked out to the rental car.

When they got back to the Marriott, she turned on the shower and returned to the room to leave her clothes. He followed her lead and got into his birthday suit to help her. They soaked in the shower for a long time. When they came out, she wrapped a large towel around herself and went into the bedroom. He was following her, toweling off. She stopped at the edge of the bed and dropped the towel. He steadied her by gallantly reaching around her and putting his hands on her breasts and drawing him to himself, to steady her, of course. She leaned forward and he followed her down onto the bed.

When she awakened, she was still in Lero's arms, like a pair of spoons. As she moved, he stirred. "Do you want to get up and start on the computers?" she asked.

"I was right in the middle of something when I decided to take a nap. I think I ought to finish that before we get to the computers," he said.

She felt his arm around her waist and decided she knew what he was talking about. It seemed like a fine idea.

It was dark when they awakened the second time. His arms were crossed in front of her, each hand holding a breast. She said a prayer of thanksgiving for the way he felt about her and the way she felt about him. As she moved slightly, he awakened. He reflexively gave the nape of her neck a nice juicy kiss, and said, "I love you, Jean."

She said, "I love you, too, Dan." She wriggled out of his grasps and sat up on the edge of the bed. He playfully reached around her and pulled her back to him.

Chapter 13

When they finally got up and dressed, they opened the trac phone boxes and the computer boxes like it was Christmas morning. They put all the wrappers in the bag from the kiosk and tied the top.

Each turned on their computer and tablet and plugged in the charger for each. Once each had booted originally, they inserted names and passwords and disabled the internet, WiFi features and got ready to get down to business. Lero handed Jean the thumb drive and she plugged it in her laptop. A screen came up in dark blue with white writing. "Encrypted file. Enter password." There was a blank below. Lero reached around her and typed in the password that Jefe had given him. In a couple of seconds, the screen began to show the files that would be downloaded. It was about sixteen gigabytes, so it took a while to load.

Lero put in Jefe's number on the trac phone and signaled that he wanted to send a text.

He then wrote "703 455-8989 and 703 455-9123." Then he pushed the send button.

The Cray computer at the NSA facility in Utah, recorded the message, but had no idea who the owner of the trac phone was or who the sender of the message was.

Jean said, "The files have all loaded. Do you want to load them into yours?"

"Sure," he said and took the thumb drive from her soft hand.

He plugged it into his tablet, typed the password, and it began to upload just like it did in Jean's laptop.

Chapter 14

You could tell that the wind was blowing there when he answered the phone. The old handset whistled and moaned as he answered: "Aircraft Salvage."

"Hello, I need two recently surplused airliners. Can I see your inventory on the internet?"

"Yes, Mister. Go to Aircraft Salvage Mojave.com and have a look. We have a pretty good selection just now. Let me know if you want to come and have a look."

"Okay. Thanks a lot. See you later."

"Goodbye."

Lero used his new tablet to access the internet and go to AircraftSalvageMojave.com. A nice overview of the Mojave Airport appeared with an impressive array of parked airliners. The south east corner of the Airport was occupied by the Rutan Brothers facility. They had built and flown the Voyager Aircraft around the world without landing in 1987. Lero remembered visiting with them at the big airshow at Oshkosh, Wisconsin, in an earlier time.

The inventory was accessible with a tab and when he hit the arrow on the tab, a list of aircraft appeared. Each aircraft was set up so you could view a picture and get the log data on it. He and Jefe thought that flying the aircraft from the states would be less observable than trying to locate and staff such a flight anywhere else. It would take these airplanes twenty four hours of flight time to get where they were going. Three stops probably, maybe only two. Several of the military aircraft were bigger, but they would be difficult to disguise and did not have facilities for that many passengers. This was going to be a real squeeze, and actually a short flight once they got loaded, so they needed to cram as many people into the planes as they could and scram out of Syria.

After looking at the list, Lero settled on two Lockheed Ten Eleven aircraft. They were high time, about forty thousand airframe hours, but each had engines in the middle of their useful life, and the number of cycles (landing gear retraction and extension) indicated that they had been used for long international flights. It seemed to him that the reason they had been surplused was a combination of rather high times and the arrival of more fuel efficient and more modernly equipped replacements.

Chapter 15

It was just the kind of cross country trip that Lero liked to take the Twin Comanche on. The flight planning program on his computer said that the distance was four hundred five miles, using VORs for navigation. The straight line was a little less, but went through some Military Operations Areas, which he would rather avoid.

Before dawn, he arose and dressed quietly. Jean stirred and said, "Wish I could go with you."

"What do you have on for today?" he asked.

"No appointments. The usual office work. You know, with all the running around we have to do, we really ought to think about getting someone to person the office and do administrative work."

"I agree. Let's tell Jefe and see if he has any ideas. Just put the phone on message feature and we can check it a few times a day."

"I will shower and dress if you will fix me a fruit bowl for breakfast. I wish you could scrub my back, though."

"If I scrub your back, we will not get out of here till late afternoon, much as I would love to."

"Okay, I will hurry."

In a few minutes, she came into the kitchen, tucking her blouse into her jeans."

"Is this outfit okay?"

He said, "As difficult as it is for you to look unobtrusive. I think it is fine."

He dialed a familiar number for the Flight Service Station.

"Good Morning, Phoenix Flight Service."

Recognizing the voice, Lero said, "Pappy, I need to file a flight plan."

"Okay, go ahead," came the reply.

It's IFR (Instrument Flight Rules), November seven seven seven niner papa, a PA-30 slash Alpha (the FAA designator for his Piper Twin Comanche, slash alpha meant that it was equipped with Distance Measuring Equipment and a transponder with altitude encoding), one hundred thirty knots (cruising speed), departing Davis Monthan, proposed departure time is 0300 UCT (Universal Coordinated Time, formerly known as Zulu time, based on Grenwich Meridian Time), eight thousand feet (proposed cruising altitude), over Gila

Bend (Gila Bend VOR navigation radio, about on hundred miles north west of Tucson), Twenty Nine Palms (the next VOR), Edwards (the next VOR), destination Mojave, enroute time three hours fifteen minutes, five hours fuel onboard, Alternate is Edwards, Pilot is Dan Roman, address on file, two souls on board, aircraft is red over white, Destination contact is Ernie Galvin, phone number on file.

"Okay, I got it. Have a nice flight, Dan."

"Thanks, Pappy. Have a good day."

They ate a hurried breakfast and left the house just at dawn. The Twin Comanche was waiting for them in its hangar. By the time they pre-flighted and got going, it was seven o'clock, and the tower was just going onto day shift.

"Davis Monthan ground, Good Morning. Twin Comanche November seven seven seven niner Papa at the south hangars, to taxi for west bound departure, IFR to Mojave, with information Juliet."

"Seven niner papa, taxi when ready to runway three zero. Wind is two eight zero at ten. Good morning."

At the threshold, Lero and Jean went through the before take-off check list. Everything checked okay and he turned on the transponder.

"Tower, Seven Niner papa is ready to go on three zero."

"Seven niner papa, cleared to take off, contact approach on one two six decimal six five after departure, squawk four three three five.

"Seven niner papa, roger, squawking four three three five, and we are rolling."

With the sun at its back, the Twin Comanche ate up the runway and climbed to the west.

"Twin Comanche seven niner papa, contact Departure on one two five decimal five zero."

"Twin Comanche seven niner papa, over to Departure, good day."

"Departure, Twin Comanche seven seven seven niner papa with you climbing through three thousand."

"Twin Comanche seven seven seven niner papa, good morning, climb to eight thousand feet, report reaching, fly two eight five initial heading, cleared to Tonapah."

"Seven niner papa, roger."

As the carpet of western desert unrolled before them, they climbed through five thousand feet. Lero had reduced power from take-off power to climb power and held it there for now. The plane continued to climb at a rate of nine hundred feet per minute. As they leveled off at eight thousand feet, Lero called Departure, "Departure, seven niner papa level at eight thousand, receiving Tonopah."

"Roger Seven niner papa, traffic above you at your one o'clock, ten miles, a KC-135, descending out of ten, one zero, thousand for Davis Monthan."

"Seven niner papa is looking for the traffic, has the traffic at our one o'clock."

"Maintain contact with the traffic, seven niner papa, report passing or loss of contact."

"Seven niner papa, roger."

"I see the Gila Bend VOR. It's amazing how far you can see in the west, isn't it?" said Jean.

"Yes, the air is so much clearer out here. That VOR is still fifty six miles away, according to the DME. (Distance Measuring Equipment)"

"Seven niner papa, contact Albuquerque Center now on one two five decimal six five, good day."

"Thanks, approach, seven niner papa over to center."

"Albuquerque Center, Twin Comanche Seven Seven Seven Niner Papa, with you level at eigth thousand."

"Roger, Seven Seven Seven Niner Papa, proceed as filed, maintain eight thousand."

"Wow," said Jean, "we are almost to Gila Bend. The DME shows twenty six miles."

As they reached about fifty miles past Gila Bend, center called, "Seven niner papa, contact Los Angeles Center now on one three three decimal seven five."

"Roger Center, Seven niner papa over to Los Angeles Center, good day, thanks."

In an hour and a half they could see Edwards Air Force Base in the distance with its long parallel runways in the dry lake.

"Seven Niner Papa, contact Edwards Approach now on one one niner decimal two five, good day."

"Seven Niner papa over to Edwards Approach, thanks, good day."

"Edwards Approach, Twin Comanche Seven Seven Seven Niner Papa."

"Seven niner papa, you are cleared direct to Mojave, fly heading two eight zero, descend and maintain three thousand feet."

"Seven niner papa, roger, out of eight thousand for three."

"This is really great," he said. "We can get a really close up look at Edwards on our way."

"It looks so big," she said.

"It really is big," he said. "Those runways are fifteen thousand feet long."

In a few minutes, Lero reported, "Edwards, seven niner papa is level at three thousand."

"Roger, seven niner papa. Direct to Mojave now, fly two eight five."

"Roger, Edwards, seven niner papa two eight five, has Mojave in sight."

"Seven niner papa, contact Mojave tower now on one one eight decimal six, good day."

Chapter 16

When he and Jean landed, Lero taxied over to the Rutan Factory and shut down. He and she went into the waiting room and greeted the desk lady.

"Good morning, I have an appointment to look at a plane. Would it be alright if my wife stays in your pilot's lounge for a while?"

"Sure, mister. Turning to Jean, she said. "Make yourself comfortable. The coffee is fresh and so are the donuts."

Lero said to Jean, "I may be an hour or two. Will you be comfortable here?"

"Sure," she said. "There is so much to look at. Those pictures on the walls bring back a lot of memories. Dad loved working on experimental airplanes."

He gave her a little smooch and walked out into the blinding sunlight. The Aircraft Salvage office building was about half a mile to the west, so he decided to walk.

The good thing about the high desert heat was that your perspiration dried almost instantly and he was a bit hot, but dry, when he opened the door to the old metal building that housed the office of Aircraft Salvage.

"Morning," said the gent at the counter.

"Morning," said Lero.

"How can I help you?" the man asked.

"I came to have a look at a couple of the planes you have in your inventory on line."

"Which two? I will pull their files," he said.

Lero noticed that he was older, graying and walked with a slight limp. The framed military patches on the wall behind him included one that was very familiar to Lero.

"Were you in the CBI?" he asked.

"Yep. Flew the Hump a few times."

"My dad was a Flight Surgeon at Chabua," said Lero.

"I was lucky. Never wounded and never sick enough to visit sick bay, but I knew who those guys were."

"My dad was Eston Stevenson," said Lero, substituting his dad's real name for that of a friend who was at Chabua.

"He was the one who stitched up my leg. What a coincidence! My name's Quincy, he said with a broad smile extending his hand. "Nice to meet you, Mr. Stevenson.

Lero let the man continue to believe he was Stevenson.

"Were you wounded coming over the Hump?"

"Yep. Jap night fighter shot at us, but we ducked into a cloud and lost him. I did not get wounded, but cut my leg on a piece of jagged metal where a round went through the cockpit as we got out of the plane."

"Glad it was no worse," said Lero.

"Me, too. I doesn't bother me any now, but I walk with a bit of a shuffle. Let's take a golf cart out to the line. These planes are in the north west group. It is about a mile."

"Okay, I am ready when you are."

He reached over and put the old tan phone headset on the desk, so any of his co-workers who might happen in would see that it was off the hook, and picked up the two files. They went out the side door and got into the nearest golf cart.

"These golf carts make it easier to get around these big planes. People don't realize how much distance is involved, but they are grateful for the carts after they see how far it is."

"This is kinda nostalgic for me. I am a retired airline pilot. Some of the planes in your inventory were with airlines that have not existed for some time."

"Yep. Take these seven twenty sevens for instance. We have forty three here now. It surprises me how many calls we get for them, mostly from the third world."

"They were good planes." Said Lero. "I have a good bit of time in them. Always brought us home."

"The bigger planes are up there ahead," he said as they motored on.

"We have several types of the larger planes, just now. We just put them all together since there are only about nineteen just now."

Lero was always impressed with just how big the larger planes were. People who just walk onto one by an airway at an airport would be stunned to walk up to one outside and see just how massive they are.

"The first one is just there, about the sixth one in," he said.

He pulled them up to the plane and stopped the golf cart in the shade of its left wing.

"Hope you don't mind using a ladder. We don't have near enough stairs for all these planes."

"I don't mind," said Lero.

The retrieved an aluminum ladder from the shade of the fuselage and he held it for the man to go up. Once he was up, he held the ladder for Lero. Lero had brought his flashlight and was glad he did. The man had a lantern type flash light that gave a good flood light to the interior.

"Let's do the flight deck first," said Quincy.

"How long has the plane been sitting?" asked Lero.

"Let's see," he said as he opened the file.

"This aircraft arrived last February eighth, so it has been here three months and a few days."

"Good," said Lero as they went into the flight deck and sat down at the controls. The instruments were all in order and up to date. The yoke and other movable parts were shop worn, but not damaged at all. After checking each instrument, Lero said, "Let's check out the passenger compartment."

They walked back the right aisle and came forward the left aisle. The seats were in pretty good shape, considering. The galleys were all equipped with stainless hardware and vessels and they looked good. Lero saw no flaws that would disqualify the aircraft.

He said, "Let's have a look at the undercarriages," and they went back down the ladder, each holding it for the other. He put the ladder back where Quincy has gotten it.

Using Quincy's flood light, they peered into each wheel well. No hydraulic leaks showed and all the pivot points looked good. The tires were more worn on the main gears, as one might expect, but they had plenty enough tread left for what Lero had in mind.

"This one is definitely good enough. Let's check the other one," Lero said.

They climbed back into the golf cart and went four planes down the line. This Ten Eleven was painted a dark red, whereas the first one he looked at was a dark blue. They did the same ladder thing and gave the plane a thorough look over. It was not as fresh as the first one. The airframe had forty eight thousand hours and eleven hundred gear cycles more than the first plane. It was older, but it was solid. After a good look over, Lero said, "This one will do, too. Let's go back to the office and talk."

Once they got back and sat down across the desk from each other. Mr. Quincy put the files down on the desk. He opened the first one and said, "The asking price on the first one, the blue one, is Seven hundred fifty thousand. The red one is Seven hundred, even."

Lero asked, "Mr. Quincy, based on everything you know about these planes and your experience, is that a fair price?"

"I think so, Mr. Stevenson. These planes are consigned to us and the owner sets the price, but based on the market, here and world wide, these seem fair to me. We get a commission based on the sale price, but that comes out of the seller's money.

Lero said, "I would like to leave a deposit on each aircraft. If we take them, you can use that as part of the purchase price and if we don't take them, you can keep half of the deposit for your trouble."

"That is not really necessary, Mr. Stevenson. We will refund your deposit if you don't take the aircraft within fifteen days. When you want to close the deal, you can wire transfer the money to our account. Most folks don't like to carry checks even for that much money."

"Would Five thousand be enough to hold each plane for fifteen days?" asked Lero.

"Sure, that is fine. I will get you the bank number and the account number to send the money to, if the deal goes through."

Lero reached inside his shirt and handed Mr. Quincy two packages of Hundred Dollar bills.

Quincy thanked Lero and glanced at the bills just long enough to see that each package had a wrapper around it indicating that it contained Five Thousand dollars. He could count it carefully later, but now he felt he needed to be friendly and accommodating.

He got out a tablet and wrote out two receipts for Five Thousand Dollars each.

"How do you want the receipt to read," he asked.

"Make them to Keros Transport, LLC," and he spelled Keros for Mr. Quincy.

Quincy checked his work, then tore out the original of the receipts and gave them to Lero.

"I could tell you knew your way around these aircraft, but it is not often that we make a deal so quickly."

"It went very smoothly, Mr. Quincy. The planes were exactly as represented. Once the figures were okayed and the walk around went well, there was no doubt that these planes will do just fine. Do you want to do the closing here?"

"Yes, I will have the FAA forms ready and our accountant from Los Angeles will be up for the closing."

"Good. I may not be at the closing, but whoever comes will probably bring crews with him or her for both planes. Can we arrange fuel and other servicing here?"

"Sure, we can arrange fuel. Let us know what other consumables you want on board and we will take care of that, too. Here is my card. Call during normal business hours and we always have someone here in the office.

They stood, and Lero said, "Nice doing business with you, Mr.Quincy."

Quincy said, "Same here. Come back any time you are in the area."

Lero went out and walked back to Jean.

Chapter 17

"Coastal Aviation, Morgan speaking."

"Mr. Morgan, your company was recommended to me by the fellows at Air Salvage at Mojave."

"Yes, sir. How can we help you."

"I need two crews to relocate two Lockheed Ten Elevens from Mojave to Mumbai."

" That will mean four pilots and two engineers."

"That's right. Can you give me a bid or an estimate?"

"Yes, sir. It will take a day or two. How can I reach you, sir?"

"Call me at 800 583-2007."

"Whom should I ask for, sir?"

"Ask for Mr. Stevenson."

"Alright. Thanks for calling us. I will call you back."

Chapter 18

"Hello."

"May I speak to Mr. Stevenson, please?"

"Yes. Just a minute."

"Hello, this is Mr. Stevenson."

"Mr. Stevenson, this is Morgan at Coastal Aviation in Fort Lauderdale."

"Yes, Mr. Morgan. Thanks for a calling."

"I have an estimate for you for your ferry job. Do you want me to email or fax it to you?"

"Yes, you can fax it to me at this number. As soon as we hang up, I will switch it to fax. But, go ahead and read me the estimate, please."

"Okay. Dear Mr. Morgan. Thank you for your request for an estimate to fly two Lockheed Ten Eleven aircraft from Mojave to Mumbai, India. This project will necessitate four pilots and two engineers. We pay our pilots the going rate for airline pilots and engineers make approximately eighty percent of that amount.

Your project will entail our crews' travel from their present locations to Mojave, first of all. We will fly our crew to LAX by regular air lines. They will need a rental car and will be at least two over nights in or near Mojave. They will want a day to check over the aircraft and take them for test flights. We assume that you will arrange for fuel and other consumables at Mojave.

We plan to make the flights in three stages: Mojave to Midway; Midway to Manila, and Manila to Mumbai. We would like to have a week to complete the project.

Do you want me to read the itemization, too?"

"Sure, go ahead, if you don't mind," said "Stevenson."

Six airfares to Mojave, Two thousand eight hundred dollars,

Rental car at Mojave, Two hundred dollars,

Six times two overnights in Mojave Area, Eleven hundred dollars,

Sixteen hours for pilots and engineers, ground time for prep and check out, Ninety six hundred dollars,

Thirty five flight hours, including test flights for pilots, times four, one hundred forty hours, twenty one thousand dollars,

Thirty five hours, including test flights for engineers, times two, one hundred seventy hours, Eight thousand four hundred dollars,

Six overnights in Mumbai, Twelve hundred dollars,

Incidental spending money for pilots and engineers on international trip, Three thousand dollars,

Air fares from Mumbai to LAX, Nine thousand dollars,

Overnight in LAX, Nine hundred dollars,

Air fares home for pilots and engineers, Four thousand eight hundred dollars,

Bookkeeping fee for flight plans, estimates, and office time at Mojave, Two thousand dollars.

The total for the project is Sixty Three thousand Six hundred dollars."

"That seems very reasonable under the circumstances, Mr. Morgan. Let me get approval and I will call you back. The customer's name is Western Air Transport, LLC. Is that alright?"
Yes, sir. That will be fine. I will send the fax as soon as we hang up."

"Okay. Thanks for calling so promptly. See you later."

"You are welcome. Have a good day."

Chapter 19

"Jean, you are the only one who knows about this project who has the electronics and communications expertise to run the whole show. I want you to be aboard the Poseidon aircraft off the coast when the big event takes place. Because of the secrecy, we will probably stage those flights from Diego Garcia."

"Wow, you really know how to put a lot on a girl on the first date, don't you?" Jean parodied a line from a seventies movie. "I guess with a plane load of experts, I will be able to carry it off."

"Ground communications will probably be the biggest challenge. We don't know, as of now, whether they will be using cell phones or radios. We will probably have to parachute a technician into the area with a cell repeater if they use cell phones. If we use radios, particularly air band, we will need you to work out codes for any anticipated activity."

"I'm sure I will need you and Jefe to help me add to the list, but I will get to work on it."

"I am going to need good quality overflight photos of all the airports in Syria, so we can view them to choose one or more, too. I will get the guys at the Overhead Research Bureau to provide those. Once we narrow the choices down to two or three, we will need 'on the ground' analysis about the current situation so we can decide how best to get all the passengers together. They will need training, too, about boarding hurriedly. This will be a scramble. They will have to board all their people very quickly, so we can get them out of there."

"Why don't we go get lunch at Sonic and talk about it in the car?" she asked.

"Good idea. I like cuddling with you while we eat."

The white Grand Cherokee with its medium tinted windows afforded them just the right amount of privacy at the drive in restaurant. Lero kept his right hand on her left breast to steady her as she fed him french fries and his drink. At least once during each meal at Sonic, he leaned over and gave her a big juicy kiss on the neck.

He was so thankful for Jean. There was never enough.

Chapter 20

Lero had not ridden on a New York subway in several years. The limo dropped him off at the front of the Essex House on Fifty Fourth Street. He decided to walk a bit and ride the subway. It was cleaner than he remembered. The fares were up a bit, but otherwise it was familiar. He got off at Thirty Fourth Street. The building he was going to was a block and a half away.

The lunch room was just off of the main atrium. Tarek was waiting for him in a booth near the rear. They had not met before, but he looked like his picture.

Lero said, "New York looks the same," and smiled.

"Yes," he said, "The subways run on time, though."

Now they each knew who they were really talking to.

"Tell me about your project," said Lero.

"We have assembled a group of people, most of whom do not know anyone else, except the family units. There are embassy personnel from the U.S., employees of the governments of countries bordering Syria, some surveillance personnel from Israel, Christian ministers and leaders, former Syrian politicians and their immediate families, some people who want out of Syria and won't give much personal information, but are willing to pay handsomely for the ride, the usual suspects," he said with a grin.

"None of them know how we plan to get them out. They will be told shortly before the operation that they must find their way to a specific spot after they get the word from us that the exit is about to take place. Dealing with that many people is a security nightmare," he added before Lero spoke.

"I don't have any particulars for you just now, but I want you to know that the project has moved from the thinking stage to the planning stage. We foresee that the event will take place within the next sixty days, barring unforeseen complications."

"That is good news. My people are getting very apprehensive about ISIS hit squads and traitors in their midst."

"Do you plan to orchestrate this from here?" asked Lero.

"No," he said, "I will leave here on a pre-arranged training trip. I will be just outside of the belligerent zone, perhaps just outside of the Syrian borders."

"In case you might be compromised, we will not tell you until it is a fact where the refugees will be taken," said Lero.

"That is reasonable and prudent. With pharmacological interrogation these days, if I knew the destination, they could get it from me," he said.

"Exactly," said Lero.

"The arrangement is fine with me. I just want to get those people out. Someday Syria will be free, but not before a long and bitter struggle. Assad and his Russian cronies are well entrenched. Assad's father was one of the most successful secular dictators in the middle east. He handed his country over to his son in very good shape as far as control is concerned," said Tarek.

"Bashar is no fool. He is a Western trained ophthalmologist with a western wife. He know our culture as well as he knows his own. His spies are everywhere. Life is cheap in a state of war. Lots of good people are going to disappear before this is over," said Lero. "There are so many factions and players in Syria that it will take a long time and a lot of outside influence to bring about a civilized state. I deeply regret that our country has not come to your aid sooner, but our top level people were simply not interested in confronting the Russian Bear or Assad himself, for that matter. The pacifists in the White House and Congress were so sick of foreign military involvement after the second Iraq war that they beat the drum to bring our soldiers home. We left enough military hardware in Iraq to keep them in vehicles and arms for years. ISIS evolved and is now a major regional force. We will have our hands full for a long time, but if the new President has his way, we will do what is right," said Lero.

"We hope and pray that he does," said Tarek. "I will buy a new trac phone before I go abroad, but I will call you to give you the number before I go. How many people will have my number?" he asked.

"Three. Jefe, Jean and me," Lero said. "Once the trip is on, you will not hear from us unless we have to call it off. We expect to only hear from you if you need to postpone, also," he said.

"Thank your President and your people for doing this for us," said Tarek. "I will go now. Wait for a few minutes before you leave. If you want lunch, the fish tacos are excellent. Thank you very much."

He rose and left without a sideward glance. Lero took his advice and ordered the fish tacos.

Chapter 21

Lero's plane was the last plane from Dallas Fort Worth that evening. He drove to Tucson in about an hour. Jean was waiting for him and opened the door for him as she peeked through the door peep hole. He shut the door behind him before he hugged her, but it was a nice long sweet hug.

She took him to the kitchen directly. He left his bag by the front door. She had a nice hot scrambled egg sandwich on his plate promptly. He smiled and took a big bite.

She knew that he was exhausted, so she let him sleep until noon. When he first stirred, he saw her standing beside the bed.

"Did you sleep well?" she asked. "I know you were bushed."

"Yes, I was bushed, but I must have slept almost eleven hours," he said.

"Do you feel rested enough to help me with my monthly all over moisturizer?" she teased, tilting the bottle from side to side.

"Of course, but first let me get cleaned up, so I can do a good job," he said.

"Okay," she said, "But don't take too long."

He showered quickly but thoroughly and brushed his teeth and shaved. Just as he was washing off the remaining shaving cream, he felt her arms slip around his waist.

He toweled off his face and neck and turned to her.

She was coyly squirting the moisturizer over her front. He helped to spread the moisturizer all over her while she stood in the steamy bathroom. Since she had told him that the moisturizer should be allowed some time to soak in, he put a bath towel on the bed so she could lie down and let the moisturizer soak in without staining the bed cover. She was always grateful for his help wlth the moisturizer. It took a while for her to show him how grateful she was and how glad she was to have him back home, but they were in no hurry.

Chapter 22

(Conversations in English, now)

"Cathay Pacific Airlines, how can I direct your call?"

"Operations, please, pilot scheduling," Mr. Trevette responded.

"Very good, sir. Just a moment, please."

"Operations, Thorndike speaking."

"Good morning. I am Bruton Parrish of Worldwide Tours. I wonder if I could speak to someone about hiring four of your furloughed pilots for about three weeks of charter work in Seven Forty Sevens."

"I will connect you to Pilot Scheduling, sir. We have no objection to our furloughed pilots taking charter work. It keeps them current. Just a moment."

"Scheduling, Franklin," came the next voice.

"Mr. Trevette" repeated his request to Franklin.

"Sure, we have about twenty six seven forty seven pilots on furlough just now. I am sure they would appreciate a little work. Would you like to contact them directly or through us?"

"I would be glad to contact them directly. You guys are busy enough," said "Trevette."

"Okay. Give me a minute and I will have you some names and numbers."

In five minutes, "Mr. Trevette" had four names and European telephone numbers.

"Cooking with gas," he thought to himself as he wrote down the numbers.

Chapter 23

"Hello."

"Good Morning, Captain Rocco, my name is Andre Trevette. Do you have a minute?"

"Yes, Mr. Trevette, how can U help you?"

"Your name and number were given to me by the Scheduling Officer at Cathay Pacific. I asked him if he could give me the names of some furloughed pilots that I might hire for a short term of employment."

"That is right. I am on furlough and have been for a month and a week."

"My tour company is bringing a large group to Europe for a conference involving the possible alternatives in the treatment of the refugees from the Civil War in Syria. I need four pilots to fly two ten elevens over a three week period so these people can go to various places in the middle east to confer with local leaders about possible solutions to the refugee crisis. Are you still current in a Lockheed ren eleven?"

"Yes, Mr. Trevette, I am. How many flight hours do you anticipate over this period?"

"We think the trips we have in mind will take about thirty five to forty hours of flight time?"

"What time period are you talking about?"

"Beginning on or about July eleventh, for about three weeks."

"Where would we begin the flights?"

"We would like to have you pick up the aircraft at Pierre Forwarding at Charles De Gaulle Airport and ferry them to Geneva to pick up our group, and then proceed from there. Will take care of the expenses of overnight stays, meals and incidental expenses during the tour."

"How would our pay be arranged?" he asked.

"We will give each of you an advance of one half of the estimated amount, sent to an account of your choice, and the remainder will be paid when the tour is completed. Does that seem acceptable to you?"

"Yes, how will our pay be calculated?"

"Since we can only estimate your pay grades from the annual report of Cathay Pacific, we propose to pay each of you Twenty thousand dollars for the tour. Since there will probably be thirty five flight hours over a three week period, we would want to make sure that you are compensated at least as much as if you were flying the line for Cathay Pacific in the normal manner. There may be days when you will not be needed but we want you to stay with our tour persons at those times. If all goes well, we will compensate each of you with a fifty percent bonus, because of the possibility that you may miss a recall notice from Cathay Pacific while on our tour."

"That sounds fine, Mr. Trevette."

"May I count on you then, Captain Rocco?"

"Yes."

"Very well. I will call you back to confirm when we have chosen our four pilots and get your bank account numbers, and your location to arrange your flight to Paris and give you a contact number at Pierre Forwarding. Thank you for agreeing to come on board. Oh, by the way, would you happen to know three other pilots who would be available?

"Yes, I know several. I will give you three names after I make some calls."

"Thank you, Captain Rocco. I will look forward to hearing from you."

"You are welcome, Mr. Trevette. By the way, you are also going to need flight engineers for the L-1011 aircraft. Do you want me to round up two engineers for you, too? And how may I contact you?"

"Yes, it would be very helpful if you would get two engineers as well. How much should I expect to pay them, compared to the pilots? My telephone number is 703 455 8989. Call anytime you need to."

"Thank you, Mr. Trevette. The engineers usually are paid eighty percent of pilot's pay. Is that acceptable?"

"Yes, that is fine. Thank you."

"Good to hear from you. I will call you when I have the names."

Chapter 24

The Food for Refugees office was in a store front in Brooklyn. On one side was an Italian Restaurant and the other side, a liquor store.

Lero crossed the two lane street in the middle of the block and entered the old wooden double doors of the store front. There were four desks in the main room, each facing a central aisle of sorts. The young man at the first desk on the left asked, "May I help you, sir."

"Yes. My name is Andre Trevette. I would like to speak to the manager, please."

"He has someone in with him just now, sir. I will buzz him to tell him you want to see him."

"Thanks," said Trevette, as the young man reached for his telephone.

There wasn't any waiting or sitting room, so Trevette stood in the middle of the aisle to wait. In a few minutes, the door to the office at the rear opened and two men came out. One came toward the front door. As he approached Trevette, he courteously nodded and Trevette returned the nod.

The man who then approached Trevette was dark haired, balding, but only about thirty five years old. He extended his hand and said, "I am Mr. Mansour, the manager. How can I help you?"

"I am Andre Trevette, Mr. Mansour, my charity would like to arrange to make periodic contributions to your cause."

"Wonderful. Step into my office and let's discuss it."

Chapter 25

As he usually did, Jefe started his desktop computer as he took off his coat and prepared to get his office day under way. He had instructed all employees that he could be emailed at DirectorHB@CIA.gov. There were very few times when people took the opportunity to send him a direct email, but this morning, there was one in the queue.

The letter showed a picture of the sender, a comely woman who looked about forty, named Patricia Anderson. The message read, "I have something I think you need to see. I would appreciate an appointment." Before he opened his paper mail, he emailed back, "Would it be convenient to come about 10:30?" That time interval gave her enough time to walk or ride a golf cart from wherever she might be on the Langley campus to his office before 10:30.

As he was opening the third envelop of interoffice mail, his screen showed an incoming email.

"Ten thirty will be fine. Thanks." He busied himself in reading to try to bring himself up to speed in his new position. The task was daunting. So much to learn, so little time.

She appeared in the outer office promptly at ten thirty. He could see her through the window panel beside his inner office door. His office secretary buzzed him on the intercom.

"Ms. Anderson, to see you sir. She didn't have an appointment as far as I can tell."

"It's okay, Mildred. Show her in."

He rose from his desk chair and went toward the door to greet her.

"So nice of you to see me so quickly, sir. I am Elaine Anderson," extending her hand.

"Nice to meet you. Please have a seat."

Once they were seated, he said, "What was it that you wanted to see me about?"

"It is a very touchy matter, Director. I don't feel comfortable talking about it here."

"I see," said Jefe. "Why don't you meet me for lunch?" He scribbled an address on one of his cards and handed it to her. She glanced at it and nodded.

"Thanks again for seeing me so quickly. Welcome to Langley, sir."

"Thank you for your loyalty, Ms. Oglethorpe. Have a nice day."

She left as quietly as she arrived.

Chapter 26

Later, at the Air and Space Museum, she approached him at the Enola Gay exhibit.

"It is beautiful, isn't it?" she asked.

"Yes, beautiful and deadly. My father was a B-29 pilot and was on Tinian when they bombed Hiroshima and Nagasaki. He knew Tibbits well. Looking at this plane brings it all back. Dad only talked a bit about his service time, like most of the guys."

"Is this a good place to talk? I need to show you something," she said.

"Why don't we look for a spot that is better and more secure," he said. Stay here a few seconds after I leave, then follow me," he said.

She nodded. He turned right and slowly walked away, pausing a few times to look up at the Enola Gay. On the far side of the room, he noticed a small alcove behind an engine exhibit. He walked past it and noticed that is was an inset in the wall of the exhibit hall, about eight feet square, with walls on three sides and open to the main gallery on the other side. He walked around the exhibit of the R3350 Pratt and Whitney engine and ducked into the alcove after he checked to see if anyone nearby was observing. He waited a few minutes for her. She was careful about being observed, too, and in a few minutes walked into the alcove.

"I am in the overhead observation office. We get all the feeds from the satellites and drones and aircraft for analysis. I know it is a breach of protocol, but Warren (the Director) told me that he suspected that the Assistant Deputy Director of Clandestine Services, Alton Cummings, was feeding information to some outside interest. Since I am in the Overhead Office, he asked me, on the QT, to keep my eyes open for anything. Since Warren had told me that Cummings was fond of kayaking on the bay, I re-tasked one of our Reaper drones to fly over the bay on its daily travels. After several tries, it picked up what we think was Cummings out on the water. We probably would have missed it if the drone had not been equipped with a wide band scanner on its radio interception gear. It appeared like Cummings was leaving a small weighted container attached to a float with a short range low frequency beacon attached. I told Warren about it just before he left on the Japan trip and he said we would put something into operation after he got back and for me to continue to check the overhead intel from that area to see if there were a pattern in Morgan's behavior. I theorized that Cummings texted the GPS coordinates of the drop to his pickup person so they could find the capsule easily."

"This is very disturbing and very valuable information, Ms. Anderson. Does anyone else know about this but you and Warren?"

"I have told no one. I don't know if Warren has shared it with anyone."

"Alright. Let's keep this just between us. I will put something together and will get back in touch. Give me your cell phone number, please. Put mine in yours, too. Mine is 703 226-4566."

She quickly put the cell number he gave her into her phone and then said, "My number is 703 492-1787."

"We must be very careful," he said. "As Acting Director, I will be the target of lots of efforts to hack my phone and computer. When you propose a meeting, just say, 'Report being transmitted by email,' then say 'this afternoon' and I will know to come here. If you want to meet after 5 PM, "say 'overnight' and I will meet you at the International House of Pancakes on Arlington Boulevard in Alexandria at 8 PM."

"Alright," she said. "Thanks for your help. Please let me know as soon as you can about Warren."

"I will, and thanks for your help, too," he said and watched her walk out past the engine exhibit and out of sight.

Chapter 27

"I met an interesting woman today," Jefe said.

"Oh, no, you are dumping me now that you are the Director," said Alita, with a feigned look of desolation on her face.

"No such thing, sweet pants. This is business. This woman may have important information for us and when I am out of the area, I want you to meet with her if she needs to meet to transmit information quietly."

"I am so relieved, Harry. I have been concerned about a rush toward you. You know how goosey some women get around powerful men," she mimicked as she came around the table and gave him a hug.

He smiled broadly and said, "You know, I have not been very interested in other women since you kissed me on the front porch on our first date. I still get a surge thinking about it."

"That was as memorable for me as for you, dear," she said as she wrapped her arms around his neck. They kissed and fondled for bit and then he said, "I think it is pretty safe to converse here, but once we move to a more long-term place, we must be very careful what we say. I am sure that our quarters will be surveilled."

"I guess it goes without saying. Do you think we will be able to detect any cameras or microphones?"

"I will have the place swept often, but they now have a device that uses a laser beam against a window pane and can pick up interior conversations from a long distance. We will have to whisper a lot. I will ask the guys to install countermeasures, but the problem is that we don't know which of these people might be a problem."

"I will be careful, but it gives me a creepy feeling to think that people are watching us. You know how much I dislike wearing clothing when we are alone."

Jefe smiled and pondered what she had just said a while before he changed the subject back to the woman he had earlier described.

"This woman I mentioned, before, is an employee. She emailed me that she had a concern and I invited her to visit me at the office. She was reluctant to discuss her matter there, so I met her at the Air and Space Museum and we talked in a small alcove that seemed private enough, over by the Enola Gay display. Once we were alone, she let her professional demeanor slip and sobbed a bit as she told me that she is and has been involved with Director Schmidt for some time. She is distraught that he is missing and worried sick. She is trying to keep a stiff upper lip, but is it really about all she can stand."

"Oh, the poor woman," said Alita. "Are either of them married?"

"Schmidt is divorced. She did not elaborate on her marital status. I will find out later," he said.

That is the personal side of what she told him. Jefe did not tell Alita the rest of the details about the conversation.

They did not often discuss Harry's business, but one evening, after the encounter with Elaine Anderson, Alita asked him about the FSB. She had been reading a report on the internet about Soviet intelligence and wanted his perspective.

"Well, it all started when Nickolai Lenin created the Cheka, his own secret police to whip people into line and keep them there. It was a scourge and very brutal. Probably due to pressure from outside, after he died, the new leaders changed the intelligence apparatus to the NKVD, with not only secret police duties, but espionage and propaganda units. Then, after the Stalin era, and its massive purges and assassinations, the new leader, Nikita Kruschev, a senior Army General who led the Russian response to the siege of Stalingrad, changed the organization to the KGB, retaining all of the jurisdictions of the old NKVD, but adding cryptography and counterespionage. It stayed pretty much the same until Boris Yeltsin became Premier. He was the most western influential leader in recent Russian history and used his knowledge of the west to make substantial changes, many of them very liberal for a Russian. Late in his tenure, he chose Vladimir Putin from the cadre of officers in the intelligence service and asked him to become Yeltsin's successor. Yeltsin knew that his health was deteriorating and he hand-picked Putin. Putin was a great choice. He was a former fighter pilot, cocky, like a lot of fighter pilots are, and cunning, too. He was highly intelligent and had the requisite ruthlessness to manage the growing Chechyn, Georgian and Uzbek insurgencies. He pretty much orchestrated the response to the Georgian revolution, too. The Russians learned that they had another iron handed leader in those years. There were many casualties, but we get very poor information about numbers, as you might expect.

Anyhow, Putin, like most of his powerful predecessors, restructured the intelligence community of the Soviet Union and watched with dismay as the Soviet Union collapsed in 1991. He has dedicated his energy to solidifying the Russian economy and securing its borders, as well as dealing harshly with the Chechyns, Uzbecks and Georgians.

His intelligence creature is called the FSB and incorporated the best parts of the old IKS Institute of Cryptography and Protection of Information. His people are constantly on the lookout for talented geeks and computer whiz kids to recruit.

Somewhere along this period of time, Putin and the rest of the Politburo oligarchs decided to rename the entire apparatus the SVR, the Foreign Intelligence Service, which is its present name. Approximately fifty two thousand people work for the SVR all over Russia and in its diplomatic corps abroad. It is basically divided into the SVR which is the civilian external intelligence service and the GRU, which is the military's main intelligence agency. These people are not as dogmatic as the former Soviet guys, and they are more wed to the concept of the Rodina, the mother land, than to strict Communism. Nowadays, they are much more subtle and difficult to detect than before. All of these people bear close watching. They are dangerous and will kill instantly to protect their identities."

Chapter 28

"General Alliluyev to see you sir," said his aide, Colonel Vashinsky.

"Very well, show him in," said Vasily Pugachev, the head of the FSB.

Pugachev always deplored the showy and ornate office he and his colleagues had "inherited" from the old Soviet Union. They were so showy and impractical that it was a constant source of irritation. He came from behind his huge desk and shook the hand of his friend Alliluyev.

"Ah, Uri, so good to see you again. Come, have some tea and sit."

"Thank you, Vasily," said Alliluyev.

Once seated and with a saucer and tea cup in his right hand, Alliluyev said, "Vasily, that matter I spoke to you about last week has continued to deteriorate. I am very apprehensive that our man may be detected and apprehended in the near future. I think we need to act and I came to seek your guidance. How do you think we should handle the situation?"

"I am sorry to hear this. He is one of our most productive agents and has been very loyal. His placement leaves us very few options. Since you are so convinced that his discovery is imminent, we had better take action promptly."

"Do you want me to put something together?" asked Pugachev.

"Yes, reluctantly, I agree with you. Something must be done. If you cannot extricate him quickly and quietly, take more stringent measures. Put your best people on it, and the fewer who know about this the better."

Pugachev rose slowly and put his saucer and cup on the corner of General Pugachev's desk.

As they walked to the door, Pugachev patted his old friend on the shoulder and said, "Don't worry about this, Yuri. I am sure it will work out alright."

"Thank you, Vasily. I appreciate your guidance. See you soon."

Chapter 29

On a foggy morning in early April, Alton Cummings walked from his car to the boat house. It was early enough that the fog had not yet burned off the bay. He opened the garage door of the boat house and lowered his kayak into the water. It took him five or so minutes to slip on his wet suit and get his gear ready, then he carefully stepped into the kayak and unclipped the mooring cord. He pushed the garage door opener as he left and the door quietly closed behind him. These were his treasured moments of solitude and he paddled slowly in the almost calm water. A half mile was a good work out and he stopped to rest before he went back. He clipped the cord of the paddle to the thwart and got out his lunch box for a snack.   There was only one pastry shop that made crullers like he liked them in the area. He liked cakey crullers with just enough icing. After he finished the first one, he got out his thermos bottle and poured himself a cup of coffee. There was no boat traffic in sight and it was completely quiet. He sat the cup on the deck in front of the cockpit and got out his message drop device. It was a foot long section of white PVC pipe with a cap bonded onto one end and a screw-on cap on the other. Attached to the screw-on cap was a cord about two feet long, with a clip on the end. He had fastened a black cylindrical transmitter there, with a styrofoam float that would hold the transmitter just at the surface with the PVC pipe and its anchor just below that. The anchor, just a large fishing weight, really, tied to a cord on the other end of the PVC pipe, would hold the whole apparatus in the water so that the transmitter would be only about an inch above the surface. The battery in the transmitter would last a day at most. He turned the transmitter on and reached over the side to lower the whole thing into the water. Just as he had lowered the whole apparatus into the water and his hand was just into the water, a black gloved hand seized his wrist. He was completely surprised and shouted in fright. The hand held onto his wrist while another gloved hand slipped a nylon tie wrap onto his wrist and jerked it tight. The underwater diver then pulled the plug on the flotation device that was supporting the cement weight in the water. As the anchor became heavier as air was escaping from the flotation device, Cummings felt the full weight of the cement filled five gallon can. He screamed in fright and panic. He never saw more than the hands of the diver. He held onto the kayak as long as he could, but in a few moments, the weight pulled him and kayak over and he was pulled under by the weight and disappeared into the water of the bay. After he was gone, the diver surfaced, put the drop apparatus into a net attached to his waist belt and swam toward the boat that was rapidly approaching from the west.

Chapter 30

The cell phone buzzed beside Jefe's bed. As he answered it, it showed the time as 2:43 AM.

"Yes," he said.

"Sir, sorry to wake you, but there is a report that Alton Cummings is missing."

"Who reported him missing?" asked Jefe.

"His housekeeper noticed that he did not return from his morning kayaking on the bay. We immediately put a crew on it. They found his kayak floating upside down about a mile off shore from his home. We alerted the authorities and they are mounting their own search."

"Did he have family? Have they been notified?" asked Jefe.

"Cummings was divorced, but we sent a team to tell his ex-wife because she has custody of his teen-aged children."

"This is bad and suspicious. Send someone to brief me at 0700, please. Call me back if you hear anything else, please," said Jefe.

"Will do, sir. Good night."

"More bad news?" asked Alita after he hung up.

"Yes. The Assistant Deputy Director of Clandestine Services is missing. They found his inverted kayak on the bay. The civil authorities are searching."

"Can you go back to sleep? You need your rest," she asked.

"If I have something warm and shaped like you to hold onto, I am pretty sure I can," he said.

Chapter 31

"Mid-East Ops Center, Jones speaking."

"Jonesy, this is Jankawicz at Cathay Pacific Planning. I need to file flight plans for a couple of freighters."

"Okay, go ahead, I am ready to copy."

"Both are Lockheed Ten Elevens, first one is Foxtrot Alpha Papa November Romeo Romeo. Fuel is fifteen hours. Souls on board will be three. Departing Mumbai on April twenty at twenty two hundred hours UTC. (This is Universal Coordinated Time, formerly known as Zulu time, and is actually Greenwich Meridian time.) Destination is Incirlik, Turkey. Estimated flight time is three hours forty five minutes. Equipment code is Romeo. (This means that the aircraft is equipped with area navigation system such as loran or GPS.) Read that back to me, please."

Jonesy read back the flight plan.

"Perfect, Jonesy. The other flight plan is similar, except the aircraft code is Foxtrot Charlie Delta Mike Romeo Romeo, and the departure time is one hour later."

"Okay. Anything else?"

"No, thanks, Jonesy. See you later."

"Right. Thanks for the call."

Chapter 32

The old man was sitting on a wicker chair behind the counter. A lady customer approached. When it became clear that she was interested enough in his wares to be worth it, he stood and spoke to her. (In Arabic)

"May I be of service?" he asked.

"Yes. I am looking for a bracelet for my niece for her birthday. Do you have something in white gold?"

"Yes, we have some very nice pieces. Just a moment, please," he answered. He turned and went into the back room of his small shop. Outside the bazaar teemed with activity. Lots of hurrying persons, lots of noise, lots of dust and various delightful and disgusting smells. In a moment, he returned with a shallow drawer about a foot square, lined with a dark blue velvet. He put the drawer on the counter between them and said, "These are what we have presently. Does any one of them interest you?"

"Actually, I was looking for one with a ruby and a saphire," she said.

He froze. That was the code phrase he had waited months to hear. When he regained his composure, he said, "Bracelets with rubies and sapphires are quite rare."

Now they each knew that they were talking with the person intended. Each had waited long months for this moment. His face took on a serious look. She leaned over the counter and handed him a card.

She said, "Something is going to happen. I cannot elaborate just now, but for planning purposes, how many people are involved in your group?"

"Forty eight," he said.

"Very well," she said. "Without being too specific, begin to tell them that they must prepare for a call to act. I cannot give you a time window just now, but generally prepare them to be ready to move on short notice. Tell them to bring only what they can carry and walk with."

His eyes twinkled and he smile cautiously. "Thank you," he managed.

"I will return if you think you can locate some bracelets with rubies and sapphires."

"I will do my best, madam, but they are difficult to find in these times."

"Very well. Thank you," she said and turned to leave.

Chapter 33

On a hot and dusty afternoon, she returned to the jeweler's shop. He recognized her immediately. He brought a tray of bracelets for her to look over.

As soon as she determined that they were sufficiently alone to talk privately, she said, "A bus with the number six one eight will stop at the bus stop on Prince Ali Boulevard down by the bazaar at approximately one PM on May fifth. There will be room for forty eight people. Tell your people not to bunch up, but arrive in small groups. The group leader should speak a code word to the driver when he has all of his people on board. Once the bus is under way, the driver will brief the passengers on the plan. If there are any problems before hand, the bus will not stop or will leave before filling. If the bus does not arrive within half an hour of the appointed time, your people should disperse and we will try again later."

"Thank you," he said. "We will do as you instruct."

"Very well. Good luck," she said, and she turned and left the shop.

Chapter 34

The market in Homs was packed. Dust filled the air. The noise was considerable as people tried to talk over the shouts of the merchants. It was just short of bedlam. It smelled alternately wonderful and terrible as the aromas of the roasting mutton and vegetables drifted about, at sometimes mixed with the smell of the barnyard adjacent to the market, not to mention the smells of the great unwashed that pressed close to buy what they wanted. At the stand of a food merchant, a lady stood in line to purchase food for her lunch. Once she had bought her lunch and looked for a place to sit down to eat, she spied a group of chairs under a tent fly that afforded some shade. She sat in a folding metal chair and balanced her plate on her thighs and began to eat. Another lady came up and asked if she minded if she sat beside the first woman. The first woman welcomed her with a warm smile. They ate in silence for a while. After they finished their plates and began to eat the fruit they had bought as a dessert, the second lady spoke.

"The fruit is especially good this year."

The other lady was jolted, but managed to retain her gaze without a change in expression.

"Yes, the dates are quite good, too," she said.

Now the second lady knew that she was talking to the person she sought and the first lady knew that the second lady was coming with important news.

"Do you eat here often?" asked the second lady.

"I usually eat her twice or three times a week, while I am shopping for food for my family," said the first lady.

"Your husband, Kameel is safe in a refugee camp in Jordan. He knows we are contacting you. We are going to try to get you and your family out to join him. I cannot give any details just now, but please get yourself and your children ready to travel. I will bring final instructions when I come next. If you could arrange to eat here next Wednesday, I may come then. I will try to come on a Wednesday after that, if I do not come next week. When you are being transported, bring only what you can comfortably carry. I must go now. See you soon."

The first lady sat in stunned silence as she watched the other woman disappear into the dusty crowd of the bazaar.

Many of the homes in Homs had upstairs rooms where the male leaders of the family could hide in times of danger. Kaseem Apgar was sitting quietly, watching Al

Jazeera on a portable, battery operated set. His cell phone buzzed. (Conversation in Arabic)

"Hello."

"Sir, this is Jaffar Al-Akbar. May we speak for a moment?"

"Yes. I know who you are. How can I help you?" asked Apgar.

"I am not calling to request help, but to offer it, sir," said Jaffar.

"I don't understand," said Apgar.

"I need to speak to you face to face. Can you meet me on the north side of the Beni Kedem mosque at eight this evening, alone?"

"I could do that. How will I recognize you?" asked Apgar.

"I will have on a black cap and a red scarf," answered Jaffar.

"Very well. See you then."

"Thank you, sir. See you then."

The first thought Apgar had was that it could be a trap set by the Syrian government to take him into custody.

From such capture, he would very probably never be seen or heard from again. He decided to approach the mosque from the north and get a look around before he revealed himself. He got his gear ready: a pair of black, lightweight binoculars, his trusty Browning Hi-Power nine millimeter pistol, a small LED flashlight, his black tactical trousers and his black light weight jacket. He chose a dark blue Greek style cap. With this clothing, he could blend in and at the same time have the protection of dark colors over all. He would wear his black Nike cross trainer shoes, too. Once all of that was ready, he made a light dinner of hummus and spelt bread while he continued to watch Al Jazeera for regional news.

At seven thirty, he turned out the light in his room and the rest of the lights in the lower floor of the house as he exited. It was half a mile to the mosque and he set out at a firm pace to arrive on time.

He passed no one he knew nor that presented a threat on his walk. People on the streets and back alleys of Homs were very wary at night. There were no solitary women on the streets. Most of the people out at night were groups of two or three men. He made the half mile in good time and found a large dumpster to stop behind so he could survey the area with his binoculars. There were two men nearby that he thought would be sentries for Jaffar. There, also was Jaffar, leaning against the wall that surrounded the mosque. If this were a trap, there were no obvious signs of it. There were no suspicious vehicles that might contain a large enough group of men to might make his escape impossible. After observing for a few minutes, he decided to take the risk and walked out from behind the dumpster and closed the last hundred yards of his approach.

As he grew close, Al Akbar looked up and waited for Apgar to join him leaning against the wall.

"Thank you for coming," Al Akbar said.

"You said you had something for me. Perhaps it is I who should thank you," said Apgar.

"I am instructed to tell you that there will be an effort soon to evacuate you and up to fifty of your friends and followers and fellow opposition leaders to a safe haven. I cannot be specific now, but I am told to relay to you to be ready on short notice. You have authority to involve up to the fifty people, as you choose. Transportation will be arranged from specific meeting spots. Tell your people to bring only what they can carry and move about quickly. I will be back in touch, at least a week from now, to allow you to get your people organized. Tell them as little as possible, but emphasize to them the risk and the fact that they may not be allowed to return in the foreseeable future."

"Thank you, Kaseem. I will get my people ready. I realize that you and your people are taking a substantial risk helping us. Thank you."

"We are glad to offer this opportunity to you. Your leadership will help us rebuild our country if we get the chance. A number of my people will be going as well. We are working with a discreet group from a large western democracy which will provide the transportation."

"I am grateful. Take care. See you later." The men shook hands quickly, but meaningfully. Apgar walked back the way he had come, being careful to observe anyone who seemed to be noticing or watching him. He slipped back into his darkened house, turned on a dim light and brought a cup of tea with him to the upper room.

Chapter 35

Jefe's trac phone buzzed in his shirt pocket. He glanced around to confirm that he was alone, then answered.

"Hello."

A familiar voice said, "I need to talk to you."

He answered, "Okay, where and when?"

"You say, I am not as closely scheduled as you."

"Okay, how about the pancake place at four?" knowing that Lero knew which one he was talking about.

"Sounds good. See you then."

At a couple of minutes to four, Jefe drove into the parking lot at the IHOP in Alexandria. He had taken precautions to assure, to the extent he could, that he was not followed.

He could not have seen the drone cruising above at eighteen thousand feet. "Sir, it looks like he is in the parking lot of the IHOP in Alexandria. Do you want me to see if we have anyone in the area?"

"Yes, let me know."

"Right."

"Dispatch, Alvarez."

"Manny, do we have anybody in Alexandria just now?"

"Let me check."

In a moment, he came back, "We have a female operative in her automobile on Hastings Boulevard, southwest bound," he said to the man.

"Ask her to head for the International House of Pancakes on Arlington Boulevard and call me with her cell phone at seven zero three four four five seven two one five."

"Seven zero three four four five seven two one five. Got it."

The line went silent.

In a few moments, his cell phone rang.

"Hello," he answered

"This is Helen Marston, southbound on Arlington Boulevard in Alexandria."

"Right, Marston. I need you to surveil a pair of men who are meeting at the IHOP on Arlington Boulevard in Alexandria. You will recognize one gent easily. Get as close as you can and use your distance mike, if you can.

Pick up what you can and record it. When they finish and you can, call me back and play the recording back to me."

"Will do, sir. I am just turning into the parking lot now."

Jefe swung into the booth seat opposite Lero.

"What is good today?"

"The blueberry pancakes with syrup and whipped cream, but I am having a glass of iced tea."

"Me too," Jefe said and pointed toward the iced tea for the waitress to indicate he wanted the same.

"I am so uneasy about security," Jefe said. "This new position takes away so much privacy. Somebody knows where I am virtually all the time. I suspect that my staff car is bugged and has a GPS in it to tell somebody where I am any time I leave in it. I don't trust it anymore and you should not, either."

"Right, said Lero. "Sorry about the creepy feeling. Would you rather get out of here and take a walk?"

"That's a good idea," said Jefe, and they rose to go. Lero left a tip on the table and paid the tab as they went out. There was a coin laundry two doors down the street. They stepped in. There was an elevated noise level, with so many machines washing and drying people's laundry, that they felt a bit more secure to converse. They sat on a bench against one wall and talked with their heads close together and in low tones.

"We are lined up for the operation," said Lero, still being very careful. "So many people's lives and the lives of their family members were potentially at risk, let alone the damage that would be done by discovery. Two separate locations. If you will put your part of the operation into action, we are good to go."

"Okay. A man named Oberlin will call you. Meet him and give him the locations and times, face to face, very carefully. He will use the code phrase, 'Looks like a good year for the Yankees' to identify himself. Your code response is: 'I have always been a Boston fan, myself.' Once you give him the locations, alert your people to the same locations and times, etc. I sure hope this goes off well."

"Me, too. I just wish I could be more helpful."

"You and Jean are much more help than you know," said Jefe. "You will need to travel to meet Oberlin. Take Jean. She will be participating in the oversight from above while you are involved with the people. Is she feeling better?"

"Yes, she seems fine. The fever is gone and her energy level has returned. I still intend to watch her carefully, though."

"Good enough. Travel safely. Report only if there are problems before the big event. See you afterwards."

Lero nodded to Jefe and Jefe rose and strode out to his car, still parked in the IHOP parking lot. As he waited to walk to his car, he notice a dark blue Ford and what looked like a woman using binoculars parked in the lot opposite Jefe's car. He watched him leave and waited for her to leave and wrote down the license number.

Jennifer Wineman answered the phone, "Records department, Wineman."

"Jenny, this is Lero. I need you to check a license number for me. Call me on this number when you can. It's a DC tag. Number one four four seven nine three. Late model Ford sedan."

"Got it. I will call you," she said as the line went silent and she turned to her console.

Chapter 36

As Miller stood waiting for the bus to Homs, he noticed a cloud of dust coming over the rise in the road from the east. In a few minutes, he saw that it was a herd of goats. There were two men leading in the front and after the goats passed, he saw a man pushing a wheeled cart behind the herd. Like many utility vehicles, motorized or not, in the middle east, it was made of scavenged parts from other vehicles. Automobile wheels and tires, mounted on an old axle. The cart was laden with metal the old man had gathered, evidently. As he got to where Miller leaned against a rock wall in the late morning sun, he paused, moved his cart to the edge of the road and lowered the end with its pushbar onto the single leg that it would stand on when not in use. He wiped his brow with his sleeve and came over to a low place in the wall and sat down heavily. The two men nodded to each other and sat in silence for several minutes. There was no one near the bus stop. After the dust and the smell of the goats blew away, it way a nice clear day.

Miller was surprised when the man spoke in English.

"I have never been fond of goat meat, myself," he said.

Reflexively, Miller answered with the phrase he had been directed to use: "I am vegetarian, myself, so it is no matter."

The local man smiled and rose from his seat on the wall and approached nearer and turned to examine something on the front of his cart.

"We make it that your people number eighty six. Is that still correct?"

"Yes, no changes," said Miller.

"Have your people arrive in a close group at one thirty AM local time tomorrow night at the Aliya Airport, north end of the runway. Wear dark clothing if possible. Only what they can carry. There will be a cut in the security fence on the north west side of the airport to facilitate your entry. Tell your people that the airplane will not shut down. There will be lots of noise and they should board very quickly. This must be done quickly and the pilots will take off as soon as your people are aboard. There will be others there, too, so tell your people not to be alarmed if more people appear at the appointed time. The premium will be on time. Get your people aboard as fast as you can. We can sort things out for more comfort after the plane is airborne."

Chapter 37

Lero phoned Jean at the temporary rented electronics laboratory in Chevy Chase as soon as he got back in the car. She answered on the third ring.

"Hello."

"I love it when you answer the phone," said Lero.

"You are so sweet to me. My telephone voice is nothing special."

"Oh, yes it is. I know where it comes from. Are you able to break away and have some dinner?"

"Sure."

"I'll be there in twenty minutes."

"Okay. I will watch for you."

She was watching out the peep hole in the front door when he pulled into the parking space. She went out directly to his car and climbed in. She scooted over in the seat and gave him one of those "I can't wait to get you home and get out of these awfully restrictive clothes" kisses. After, it took him some time to be able to concentrate enough on driving, so they just sat there cuddling for a few moments.

"I just swept this car, so I think it is safe to talk. The plan is for you to leave on commercial air for Rome Friday morning. We will be gone maybe two weeks, so we will have to pack accordingly. I will be working with the pilots and crews in Mojave and then will fly to meet you. From Rome, a military courier will motor you down to Aviano where you will board the Poseidon and I will fly out to the command center in Ovda. You will be off-shore over the Med during the operation.   Did you do okay with the taped messages?"

"Yes," she said. "It is ready to broadcast on the directional antennas. The two different broadcasts are particularized for the two airports. Our creative guys found an Arabic speaker who sounded enough like General Housa to probably fool the air traffic controllers at those airports."

"I agree. With the static that Is normal over the airband, it should not be detected. Nice work you did."

"Thanks, but how will I know when to broadcast the messages?"

"I will call you on the satellite phone or radio. I will give you the frequency to monitor before you get on the Poseidon. Jefe will be out of touch during this one, so we will pretty much be on our own. We need to protect him from interference and and discovery of the plan by our adversaries. We need to get this done to help those helpless people. In time, they will most surely be discovered and captured. I doubt if there are six people, including Mr. Murfree, above us who know the entire plan. We have compartmented all the groups as much as we can."

"I feel a heavy responsibility and I know you do, too. How many people will we be bringing out?" she asked.

"If it all goes according to plan, five hundred eighty six, mostly adults, but about one hundred twenty five children."

"Is there a lot of risk in this," she asked, soberly.

"Yes, if anything goes wrong, it could be very bad for those folks. But, to stay increases the chances that they will be discovered, in the case of the foreign agents among the group, or, in case of the opposition leaders and their families, mere discovery of their whereabouts puts them in jeopardy. Life is cheap in Syria these days. One of these planes needs only about twenty minutes to get out of Syrian airspace. The other needs about forty minutes. Those will be long minutes for them. Our guys will have some fighters loitering off the coast, but they really cannot do anything if the bad guys launch a surface to air missile."

"This is really scary for them. It makes me feel selfish to be thinking of what I want for dinner."

"A busy girl like you needs her nourishment," he said as he smooched the soft part of her neck below her ear. "We will do our best for them. That is all we can do. The rest is up to the Starkeeper."

She nodded and said, "In that case, I would like Italian for dinner, with garlic bread sticks."

"Mario's it is, then," he said as he shifted into reverse.

Chapter 38

"Hello."

"Hello, Captain Rocco, this is Mr. Trevette."

"Good evening, Mr. Trevette. Glad to hear from you."

"Are preparations going well?" asked Trevette.

"Yes, sir. I have all the pilots and flight engineers lined up. What about flight attendants? We never discussed that."

"The tour people will provide the flight attendants. Most will be regular flight attendants for the long route airlines who are on furlough like yourself. They will meet your people at Mojave before you leave so you can orient them and get them settled."

"Good. It sounds like we are getting this pretty well ready," said Rocco.

"Yes. I received your fax with the names and details about the pilots and engineers. We will wire transfer the funds to their separate accounts in the next few days. If you would, tell your people to book commercial air and plan to arrive at Mojave on the eighteenth around four PM Pacific time, please. We will have a briefing at five or so and the crews can look over their planes, get some dinner and stay overnight. We will have motel lodging arranged, so they will not need to be concerned about that. We will reimburse everyone for travel expenses when they get there. By the way, how many of the pilots or engineers are military veterans like yourself?" asked Trevette.

"As a matter of fact, they are all military veterans. We kinda stick together for special jobs like this charter and similar things," he replied.

"That is good. Do you have any other questions of me at this time?" asked Trevette.

"No," said the Captain. "I think everything has been covered. See you in Mojave."

"Good. Thanks again. See you in Mojave," said Trevette and hung up the phone.

Chapter 39

"Do you still think it is a good idea to transmit the fake message in the open to the two airports?" she asked.

"Well, it is a calculated risk. With frequency protection, there will not be another airport on those frequencies that is in range. It is highly unlikely that anyone will be monitoring those VHF frequencies, especially at the hours of the night that the broadcasts are to be made. We hope that because of the nature of the transmissions, they will be received and acted upon as we want. You will have an Arabic speaker with you on the plane to set up the exchange and then you will play the tape. After it finishes, when the tower acknowledges receipt of the message, the Arabic speaker will finish the conversation with the tower so the tower guys will be talking to a real person for the intro and the finish of the conversation and the Arabic speaker can respond to any questions from the towers appropriately. As with any subterfuge, there are risks. Once those conversations go according to plan, you will radio the two aircraft which will be approaching Syrian airspace at a proper distance to allow them to arrive at the separate airports as close to the planned arrival as possible. Once you make that broadcast, again, on a seldom used VHF air band frequency, there will be no transmissions to or from the aircraft unless there is a mission abort."

Let's listen to the message, she said:

"This is General Ali Akbar Houma of the general staff of the Syrian Arab Republic. Tonight at approximately one thirty, local time, you will receive a broadcast from an inbound flight using the call sign, 'Rafsanjani'. This is a badly needed shipment of arms from our brothers in this struggle, the Islamic Republic of Iran. They will request landing clearance. You will issue such clearance. As soon as it lands, extinguish all lights on the airport and keep them off until the plane departs. These are freight aircraft and have their own unloading equipment. They will be met by our forces to receive and disburse the ammunition and supplies. No local personnel will be required. The aircraft will be on your runway for less than an hour and will depart when they choose without running lights as security in this war zone."

"Our Arab speaker will attend to and participate in the origination of the transmission with the tower personnel and will sign off and fend off any questions after the recording is played."

Chapter 40

"Captain Rocco, this is Mr. Trevette. How are you, today?"

"Just fine, Mr. Trevette. How can I help you today?" answered Rocco.

"We have had to change the aircraft we will be using. Our earlier arrangement fell through because the rental agency could not tie up the aircraft for three weeks for us. Because we cannot change the dates of the tour, we have had to scramble to find aircraft for our tour. The best available aircraft are Lockheed Ten Elevens located at Mojave, California. Would that pose any problem for your people to ferry those aircraft from Mojave to Geneva and back to Mojave after the tour?" asked Trevette.

"Well," answered Rocco, "That will undoubtedly add some flight hours to the job, but since two of our pilots are presently located in the eastern United States and the flight engineers are also Americans, it will not present a problem."

"Good," said Trevette, "We will recalculate your compensation and expenses and add compensation for the additional flight hours and travel."

"When to you need us to be ready, Mr. Trevette?"

"We will need your people to arrive in Mojave on Friday the fifteenth about noon."

"I don't see any problem with that schedule, sir. Send me an email confirming the details so I can transmit it to our people on this end, please."

"I will be glad to, Captain Rocca. If you have any questions, you may call me at the number I gave you previously. I will see you in Geneva. Thank you very much for doing this for us and for gathering the other pilots and engineers."

"You are welcome, Mr. Rocca. I look forward to meeting you in Geneva."

Chapter 41

Jefe walked down the hall from his seventh floor office to the SCIF. (A SCIF is a Sensitive Compartmented Information Facility that is built to guard against electronic or other espionage.) The door stood open and the security guard stood aside to let him enter. Jefe courteously nodded to the guard and went inside and took a seat. In a couple of minutes, the guard admitted a man that Jefe had not previously met.

"I am Ragland, sir, from the Interception Group. Thanks for seeing me on such short notice."

They shook hands and Jefe motioned for Ragland to have a seat.

"What do you have?" asked Jefe.

"Well, as you know, Morgan went missing yesterday morning. We sent a man out to his home and he found nothing amiss in the house proper, but the kayak was missing from the boat house and it looked like Morgan had taken his morning coffee cup with him at least that far. The boat house door was closed. Our man reported this and we directed him to wait there while we sent a waterborne search team out. After a search, our men found Morgan's kayak, inverted, floating about a mile off shore of his house. There was no trace of Morgan, so we called in the regular Coast Guard to look for him. They have found nothing. The peculiar thing about this is that Director Schmidt had ordered us to keep an eye on Morgan because the Director suspected Morgan of being a mole. This is not the first time that a foreign service has tried or succeeded in inserting a mole into our organization. Our Counterespionage Division is constantly alert for these penetrations and maintains vigorous surveillance, as you know.

Morgan was divorced and his ex-wife lives in Delaware with his two teen aged sons. We have discreetly notified her that he has disappeared. I always hate to come to the Director and tell him that we have so little information, but that is the nature of things sometimes. We will keep on it, sir."

"Yes. Thank you. This is especially concerning in view of the disappearance of the other men. Any news from the search for Schmidt and the others?"

"No sir. The Navy continues to deploy over-flights and the surface ships in the area are maintaining a lookout for debris, but nothing so far."

"Do you have any information that the disappearances are connected?" asked Jefe.

"No, sir, not at this time, but we continue to entertain the possibility," said Ragland. "As you can imagine, the families are frantic, but with the event so far away, there is very little we can do to reassure them. The maintenance records of the aircraft indicate no anomalies. The personnel on board are all being back tracked. The ACARS people have provided us with a track of the aircraft, but it is inexact and only points to an area about fifteen hundred miles east of Narita."

"Alright, thanks Mr. Ragland. Keep up your efforts. Your department is the point unit on this. Keep me informed, please."

Ragland stood, and said, "Thank you, Director. We wish you good luck. Welcome aboard." He turned and left the SCIF. Jefe sat and pondered a few minutes, then left and went back to his seventh floor office.

Chapter 42

"Email

From: Alita Simpson

To: Alice Brown and Hazel Kinnard

Dear Alie and Hazel,

I took your advice after our last visit with your dad and came out here to Arizona where some of my friends had found a nice place. I stayed for a while with the McIntyres that you will remember from St. Paul's. I found a place to rent here at the Retirement Community while I looked for more permanent quarters.

One of the people I encountered among the folks who invited me out here was Harry Brubaker. You remember Harry that your dad and I went to High School with. Harry took me to the Senior Prom because your dad asked him to. Your dad had graduated and gone to Hampton Sydney for his freshman year. Harry and your dad and I remained friends ever since High School. Seeing Harry again was such a treat. He has been here in Tucson for several years and works at Davis Monthan Air Base, but he is not in the Air Force. He is a contractor and has an office there. At one of the gatherings, he asked me to have dinner with him the next evening. We spent the whole evening talking about our lives after high school and did not leave the dinner table until about ten. He told me about his ex-wife and her struggles with alcohol and her eventual death about eight years ago. Since that dinner, we have grown closer over the past months and are quite fond of each other. He has invited me to live with him in his home here and I have agreed. I wanted to tell you both about this because of the sensitivity regarding your father's condition and our mutual concern for him. Harry understands that I will be visiting your father often and that I will always make sure that he receives the best of care.

I am sure you have seen in the papers that Harry was recently appointed Acting Director of the Central Intelligence Agency by President Thompson. Harry has worked closely with Fred Thompson for a number of years and when Director Schmidt's plane went missing right in the middle of several crises, Fred turned to Harry to hold things together while they re-organize the CIA. Two Deputy Directors were on the plane with Darrel Schmidt, to there is a leadership vacuum at the head of the CIA just now.

I am living just now in temporary quarters with Harry in Alexandria, Virginia. For security reasons, I will not give you the address, but you can contact me by email or by cell phone anytime. Because of the sensitivity of his position, we must be very careful about mail, telephone and other means of communication. I will be changing cell phones and numbers often, using trac phones for security reasons. I will call you the new numbers as they are acquired. I cannot guess how long Harry will be Acting Director, but it may be months or more than a year. The CIA Director is nominated by the President and confirmed by the senate, so Fred may just wait a while and get things settled down a bit before he appoints a new Director. In the meantime, the search may locate Director Schmidt, but that seems very doubtful.

Since I am an unknown quantity to the Washington establishment and to members of the intelligence community, I will continue to use my email address and will only email you using my laptop computer. Just to be on the safe side, please do not put anything "sensitive" in your emails to me.

I want you to come to Washington and visit me and us sometime soon, but we need some time to get things organized here before that would be a good idea.

I hope you will talk this over between you and let me know how you feel about my living with Harry. Harry loves your father like a brother and would never have allowed this to take place if your dad were not in an irreversible coma. If you have any anger about this arrangement, take it out on me and not Harry. He is so good to me and insists that I keep tabs on your dad by phoning the rest home often and even going to see him. Harry has to keep in touch with some people at Oak Ridge, near your dad's place, so he comes with me sometimes. Also, Harry is so busy with his work just now, I would not want him to be distracted by a family squabble. I pray this does not upset you too much. I love you both.

Mom."

Chapter 43

"Hello."

"Well, what do you think?" asked Hazel.

"About what?" asked Allie.

"Read mom's email, then call me back," said Hazel.

"Okay. Bye."

Ten minutes later:

"Hello."

"Wow, mom really dropped a lot on us, didn't she?"

"Yes, but I have to tell you that I am very happy for her. To find happiness with Harry at this time in her life, instead of the dreary existence of daily trips to the nursing home to watch dad slowly drift away is a wonderful gift. I remember Harry pretty well, but I have not seen him in about fifteen years. I remember he has such a beautiful smile, kinda like William Holden."

"Oh, I am so glad you feel that way about it. I agree, this is wonderful for her. I guess she has had some agony about telling us. Let's just separately email her and tell her that we approve and will be very supportive. Golly, having Harry appointed Acting Director of the CIA, especially at this time, is quite a hand full, isn't it? For both of them, I mean."

"Yes. Mom is game, though. She will handle this with aplomb. I am just so glad they found each other. I dreaded having her live out her years alone and connected to dad in the nursing home. Since he is in his condition, no harm will come to him and she can be confident that she is not hurting him in any way."

"Right. Is everything okay at your place, otherwise? Will you tell Roger right away or wait a while?"

"Everything is fine here, thank the Lord. I will tell Roger tonight when he comes home. He is so fond of mom that I know he will be okay with the arrangement with Harry."

"Me, too. I will tell Sam tonight. I am sure he will be alright with this, too."

"I wish we could send her and Harry flowers or something to celebrate their coming out, so to speak, but I guess we will have to wait."

"That is so sweet. Great idea, but I agree, now is not the time. Keep mentioning it, though, we will do it sometime."

"Okay, gotta go and pick up the kids at Middle School. See you later."

"Right. Love you."

"Love you, too."

Chapter 44

"Atsuki Center, this is Rosebud four."

"Go ahead, Rosebud four. This is Atsuki."

"Search completed. Area assigned to us was covered in daylight. No debris or oil slick sighted. Ocean rather calm with one foot swells. Weather clear with good visibility. Returning to base."

"Roger, Rosebud four. Return to base."

"Captain Reynolds's office, Sergeant Findley speaking."

"Hey Fin, this is Dombrowski at the watch office. Tell the Captain that Rosebud four just reported in. No joy. No debris. No oil. Seas calm. Weather clear. Returning to base. Written report to follow."

"Will do, Dom. Thanks."

Chapter 45

The intercom on Jefe's desk scratched and then his secretary's voice said, "Sir, Mr. Marple from the Overhead Surveillance Office and Mr. Summers from the Analysis Branch are here to see you. Want to meet in the SCIF. No appointment."

"Let me have a minute. Tell them to meet me there."

In another minute, Jefe stepped out into his outer office.

"I'll be in the SCIF, Sally," he said as he strode for the door.

Four doors down the hall was the SCIF for the seventh floor. Marple and Summers were waiting for him and stood when he came in.

He nodded to them and took a seat at the head of the table. They were the only three persons in the room.

"Sir, Anthony Marple of the Overhead Office. Your office tasked us with the search for the remains of

Deputy Director Morgan. Our overhead imaging detected a boat in the bay in the proximity of Morgan's home on the eastern shore. On the morning when Morgan disappeared, that boat approached the area a mile offshore from Morgan's home and halted, then approximately a half hour later, proceeded farther east and halted again, then turned about and left the area at high speed. Based on the overhead silhouette of the craft, we followed the craft to the north and found that it entered the Mobjack bay and may have docked near Matthews, Virginia. Further surveillance and approach on foot, determined the registration number of the craft. Virginia authorities confirm that the craft is owned by Tidewater Fisheries, LLC., which is a VIrginia LLC, the only registered agent of which is given as Mikael Barron, of Alexandria. We have reason to believe this is a front organization, actually operating as an extension of some Russian agents, who are known to us.

Based on this observation, we asked the Navy to search the area within a mile radius of Morgan's boat house, with their side looking sonar. Since the water was pretty shallow in that finger of the bay, that surveillance was rather straight forward. After a day of searching, they came upon a suspicious object and put a diver into the water to inspect it. He discovered a man's body, tethered to a five gallon can filled with cement fifteen feet above the floor of the bay and about thirty feet below the surface. The body was removed and the weight retrieved. The body was taken to the State Medical Examiner's office in Richmond in a Navy ambulance. Dr. Scarpetta's report confirmed the identification of the body as that of Morgan. Since Morgan was divorced and had no other living adult relatives, we have not notified anyone. Let me now let Mr. Summers brief you from the perspective of the Analysis Division."

Jefe and Marple turned their attention to Summers.

"Sir, Andrew Summers of the Analysis Division. Based on information we received from a deeply placed agent in the Kremlin, we have reason to believe that the Russians eliminated Morgan before he would have been discovered as a double agent for the Russians. We believe Morgan provided the Russians with information about Director Schmidt's itinerary, specifically the time of departure of his return flight from Narita to the United States. Mr. Marple should continue the briefing regarding the flight."

Now, Jefe and Summers turned their attention to Marple.

"Sir, we found satellite imagery footage that shows a small missile launch just a few miles west of where we believe the Director's plane probably was as we calculate it passed over. The satellite passed out of its capability to visualize the area before any explosion of a warhead occurred, so we don't know at this time if the missile launched was going toward the Director's plane or if it actually struck the Director's plane, but we should be able to determine that once we have recovered sufficient wreckage from the plane. We also realize that we may never recover that wreckage. So that is where we are at present, sir. What are your questions?"

Jefe said, "Thank you both. What efforts are being undertaken to locate the wreckage?

"A pair of Navy Destroyers are surveying the area using side looking sonar. Nothing detected so far."

"I see," said Jefe. "Thank you for your briefings. Keep me informed please. Send a written report 'Eyes Only,' please."

Chapter 46

"Seventh Fleet Headquarters, Seaman Owens speaking."

"Seaman Owens, my name is Walter Lange. I am an American and I work here in Tokyo. I have something to report to your Officer of the Day."

"Yes, Mr. Lange. Please hold."

"Deck watch, Seaman Varney speaking."

"Seaman Varney, this is Seaman Owens at the communications desk. I have a civilian on line five who wants to make a report to the Officer of the Day."

"Right. Give me a minute."

Varney walked quickly to the Officer of the Day's office, occupied just now by Captain Leroy Thomas. His deck chief, Hogan, looked up as Varney approached.

"Chief, I have a civilian on line five who wants to make a report to the Officer of the Day."

"Wait here," said Thomas.

He went to the closed door and tapped.

"Come in," said the Captain.

"Sir, Seaman Varney from Communications wants to relay a message."

"Have him come in," said the Captain.

"Sir," said Varney, "There is a civilian named Lange who wants to make a report to the Officer of the Day. He is on line five."

"Very well, Varney. You may return to your station."

"Yes, sir," said Varney and gave a salute before he turned to leave.

"This is Captain Thomas, Mr. Lange. Sorry for the delay. How can I help you?"

"Captain, I am an American working for International Nickel and living in Tokyo. I am also a ham operator. I just heard a Japanese fishing boat, transmitting in the blind, in English. They say they have happened upon some wreckage and debris floating in the water, along with some dead bodies. They say they will maintain contact with the wreckage, but want someone to come to their aid and reclaim the bodies and release them to complete their return to their base near Yokohama. I think they said the fishing boat's name was Akagi Maru, or something like that."

"Thank you very much for calling, Mr. Lange. Pease give me your full name and address and your telephone number and email address, too."

Lange quickly gave the details to Captain Thomas.

"What frequency were they using?" asked Captain Thomas.

"Four forty eight decimal one two five megahertz, Captain."

"Can you tell me when the transmission came in?" he asked.

"It was shortly before midnight, about an hour ago," said Lange.

"Did they give any information about their location?" asked Captain Thomas.

"They only said that they were approximately sixteen hundred miles east of the Japanese coast and would wait there for a return transmission. I thought it best the you reply because of the power of your transmitter and the strength of your antenna array. My set is a feeble fifty watts."

"Mr. Lange, I cannot tell you how much we appreciate this. I will follow this up and will be back in touch with you. Please advise if you change any of your numbers."

"You are welcome, sir. Glad to help. Good day."

Thomas virtually trotted to the Communications Office. As he dashed in, the Seaman on duty at the console jumped to his feet and came to attention.

"At ease," said Captain Thomas. "Can you adjust a transmitter and receiver to four four eight decimal one two five and give me the microphone?"

"Yes, sir. Right away."

In a minute or so, he handed the Captain a hand held microphone and headset.

"Record this, Seaman."

"Yes, sir," returned the seaman.

"Fishing boat Akagi Maru, on four forty eight decimal one two five approximately nineteen hundred kilometers east of Yokohama, this is United States Navy Seventh Fleet Communications, do you read?"

The seaman had turned on the speaker as well as the recorder and the room crackled with the static on the frequency. There was no response.

"Fishing boat Akagi Maru on four forty eight decimal one two five approximately nine hundred kilometers east of Yokohama, this is United States Navy Seventh Fleet Communications, do you read?"

Still static only, then. "United States Navy Seventh Fleet, this is Japanese fishing boat Akagi Maru. Read you faintly, but clearly."

"Akagi Maru, this is Seventh Fleet Headquarters at Yokohama. Did you broadcast in the blind that you had located some debris and dead bodies? If so, is the debris from an aircraft or a vessel? Over."

"Seventh Fleet. Yes, we made the call. The debris appears to be from an aircraft. Aluminum shards with insulation backing floating. A few larger pieces and what appears to be a wing tip. We have recovered four bodies. Cannot tell now that it is night time here, whether there are more."

"Akagi Maru, are you equipped with GPS or Loran?

"Seventh Fleet, Akagi Maru has an old Loran receiver. It indicates that we are at 36 degrees, fifteen minutes, forty seconds north, by one hundred fifty four degrees ten minutes fifty five seconds east."

"Roger, Akagi Maru. Have your coordinates. Can you remain there until the United States Navy arrives? Over."

"Seventh Fleet, Akagi Maru can remain here for approximately twelve hours, but after that will have to proceed to base because of fuel concerns."

"Akagi Maru. Than will be fine. Please remain on this frequency. We will contact you as we approach. We will refuel you. Thank you very much."

"Roger, Seventh Fleet. We are glad to help. Akagi Maru, out."

Chapter 47

"Admiral Hersey's office. Commander Blake speaking."

"Commander, this is Captain Thomas, the Officer of the Day."

"Yes, Captain Thomas. How can I help you?"

"We have information on that missing aircraft and I want to ask Admiral Hersey for permission to divert some ships and make other arrangements."

"Hold a minute, Captain Thomas. I will get the Admiral on the speaker."

In a moment, Admiral Hersey came on the line:

"Captain Thomas, this is Admiral Hersey, bring me up to date."

"Sir, I received a call from an American civilian who lives and works in Tokyo. He is a ham radio operator and was listening when he heard a broadcast in the clear from a Japanese fishing boat, the Akagi Maru, reporting finding bodies and wreckage debris on the ocean surface. I want to divert a destroyer to rendezvous with the fishing boat and initiate an investigation possibly involving other ships and personnel."

"Good work, Thomas. How do you know their location?" asked the Admiral.

"They have an old Loran on board, sir," said Thomas.

"Good enough. Find out which ship is closest and divert them right away. Follow up with other craft as you deem prudent. Report your activities twice daily, please. We will handle public relations from here. We will contact CINCPAC and the Chief of Naval Operations. Please direct all inquiries to us, Captain."

"Yes sir. We will get under way immediately."

"Very well, Captain. Carry on."

"Yes, sir. Good day."

"Chief, call plot and ask them to tell us which U.S. Navy vessel is nearest to the coordinates they gave us. We will call them from here," said Thomas.

"Yes, sir," said the seaman and walked quickly to the nearest telephone. In a minute, he returned with the name, Destroyer Arleigh Burke, seventy five nautical miles east of the Akagi Maru, presently headed south west."

"Get me on their frequency and the satellite telephone, seaman," said the captain.

"Yes sir," was the prompt response, and the seaman scrambled at his computer terminal to get the information.

"Sir, they are on one forty six decimal seven five kilohertz. I have set the frequency, just pick up the headset over there and call them."

"Arleigh Burke, Arleigh Burke, this is Seventh Fleet Operations."

After a short pause, came the response, "Seventh Fleet, this is Arleigh Burke, go ahead."

"This is Captain Leroy Thomas. I have urgent orders. Tell me when you are ready to copy."

"Ready to copy Captain Thomas, go ahead."

"Proceed at best speed to latitude thirty six degrees, fourteen minutes, thirty seconds north, one hundred fifty four degrees, fifty, five zero, minutes, seventeen seconds east. Rendezvous with Japanese fishing boat Akagi Maru. Their frequency is four four eight decimal one two five megahertz.   They have located debris and bodies on the water that may be from the aircraft of the Director of the CIA which disappeared last week in that area. Take bodies and debris into custody and direct the search from your position. Advise your needs in terms of equipment and personnel to us. Acknowledge."

The chief boatswain's mate read the message back to the Captain.

"That is correct, Chief. Have your captain call on this frequency with any requests or questions."

"Will do, sir. Good day."

"Get me back on the Akagi Maru's frequency, Seaman."

"Yes, sir."

"Akagi Maru, this is United States Navy Seventh Fleet headquarters."

"Seventh Fleet Headquarters, this is Akagi Maru. Go ahead."

"Be advised, the U. S. Navy Destroyer Arleigh Burke will rendezvous with you as soon as it can get there. It is presently seventy nautical miles east of your position. They will refuel you, among other things. We appreciate your cooperation in this matter. Some token of our appreciation will be forthcoming. Advise us if there are any problems. Thank you."

"U. S. Navy Seventh Fleet, this is Akagi Maru. Acknowledge your transmission. Will look for destroyer Arleigh Burke. Thank you. Standing by."

Meanwhile on the Arleigh Burke: "Plot, this is the captain. Give us a course to latitude thirty six degrees, fourteen minutes, thirty seconds north, one hundred fifty four degrees, fifty minutes, seventeen seconds east."

"Yes, sir. Right away."

"Bridge, this is Captain Rowsey. Turn to course two six five and go to full speed ahead. I will come to the bridge to direct efforts."

"Captain, this is Lieutenant Jarvis. Wilco. Left to two six five and full speed ahead."

Full speed ahead in a destroyer is obvious to everyone on board. The whole ship hums with engine thrust and the propeller wash is considerable. The Arleigh Burke came alive in the night.

Chapter 48

The phone buzzed beside Jefe's bed.

"Hello," he answered, trying not to sound sleepy.

"Sir, the Seventh Fleet reports that a Japanese fishing boat has located debris and bodies east of Japan. The Arleigh Burke is enroute, seventy miles east of the location. No other details at this time," said the watch officer.

"Thanks, Bill. Let me know if there are any other developments."

"Will do. Get some rest, sir."

The line went silent.

Chapter 49

"Captain Fitzcharles' office, Seaman Murphy speaking."

"This is Commander Rowsey, of the Arleigh Burke. Let me speak to the Captain, please."

"Yes, sir. Hold please."

"This is Captain Fitzcharles, Commander Rowsey, go ahead."

"Sir, We are enroute to rendezvous with a Japanese fishing boat, the Akagi Maru, about fifteen hundred fifty nautical miles east of Japan. They reported bodies and debris in the water. May be from the missing aircraft with the CIA Director aboard. Would you fly a forensic team to the George H. W. Bush so we can ferry the bodies to the Bush for forensic autopsies?"

" Affirmative, we will deploy a forensic team to the Bush right away."

"Thanks, Captain. Good evening."

Chapter 50

Printer number one in the Combat Information Center of the Aircraft Carrier George H. W. Bush gave a chime and a green light lit on its top to signal that it was operating. A seaman came over and tore off the sheet and took it to the Commander of the watch.

As soon as the Commander read the message, he summoned a seaman with a hand signal and put the message in a manila envelope and had the seaman take it to the Captain's cabin.

"CIC, Commander Graves."

"Skip, set a course for the coordinates in this message. Alert Sick Bay to be ready to assist with autopsies of the victims. Tell the Air Boss to expect a COD today sometime from Atsuki."

(COD is short for Carrier Onboard Delivery, a twin engine aircraft capable of landing on the carrier, designed to deliver supplies and personnel to and from a carrier.)

"Will do, sir."

Chapter 51

Captain Rocco and two of his fellow pilots arrived at LAX on the same flight from DFW. Ogle was asked to get them a rental car while the others went to the baggage carrel to retrieve their luggage. After a lunch at the Greek Restaurant, they left for Mojave. It was about ninety miles and took them the better part of two hours. When they arrived at Aircraft Salvage, the other pilot and the engineers were waiting. They spent some time getting re-acquainted and then asked the desk man for the papers for each airplane. By this time, they had agreed on who would be part of each crew and then the desk man took the first crew out to its aircraft. In a few minutes, he returned and took the other crew out.

The men divided up in each aircraft and inspected each thoroughly. One walked around the aircraft from the ground level, with a strong flashlight. Even in the sharp sunlight of Mojave, the huge landing gear cavities were dead black and a flashlight was necessary to inspect them and look for hydraulic leaks. He found a small leak in the nose gear and made a note. Otherwise the whole aircraft checked out okay on the walk around.

Inside, Baker and Rocco were busy checking out the flight deck instruments. They turned on the avionics master to enable them to check the radios without turning on the whole aircraft electrical system. They checked the navigation radios, the communications radios, the transponder with the altitude encoder and the autopilot. All the gauges on the engineer's panel were in good working order. The fuel gauges indicated that each tank was near empty. The oil capacities in the engines indicated full. The log showed that the oil had been changed just ten flight hours ago, and three calendar months ago. The right seat navigation radio indicator did not function, but they found a popped circuit breaker. When they pushed the breaker back in, the gauge read normally. They decided to take a lunch break and talk things over and plan their flights.

There was a considerable group of cars around a particular restaurant in Mojave, about a mile south of the field. The guys decided that was where the best food was, so they parked and went in.

There were some open tables near the north wall, so they pulled two tables together. They ordered lunch from the waitress and then notice the group from the Rutan Aircraft Factory across the room. All of them knew the Rutan Brothers by sight, since Burt had designed and they both had built the Voyager Aircraft that flew around the world without refueling with Dick and his friend Jeanna Yeager piloting.

Getting down to business, Rocco asked them their opinions about the flights to Geneva. All of them except Ogle wanted to go east over the Atlantic to Europe, so they decided to go that way. That route would provide more opportunities for refueling stops and better radar. The Atlantic hops would be much shorter than the Pacific route, too.

Pierce suggested the route from Mojave to Goose Bay, Labrador, then to Edinborough, then Geneva. The guys nodded and Rocco made a note. Flying without passengers, they could top up the fuel and have maximum range. They guessed the flight time at twenty two hours.

"By the way, did everyone get paid okay?" asked Rocco. All nodded.

"Good. One less detail to worry about. I will get the meals enroute. Do you want to overnight in Goose Bay or Edinborough? We can stage our departure accordingly."

"Better food at Goose Bay," said Perkins, one of the engineers.

No one commented, so Rocco said, "Okay, when we go, we will stage for an overnight in Goose Bay. Do you have a hotel recommendation, Pierce?"

"Definitely the North Woods Hotel. Best food by far," he said.

"Okay, I will call for reservations. Do you want to take a check ride this afternoon?"

All nodded.

" We will need to check these planes out at altitude, so we had better plan on a couple of hours aloft. Does anyone have a suggestion?

Ogle said, "Since we are in the desert, I suggest we fly over to Las Vegas, land, have a nice dinner and come back. We have rooms in Mojave for overnight tonight."

Perkins said, "We will need to fly past Las Vegas to get in enough time to check everything out, including the autopilot and area navigation, but we can double back there for dinner."

Heads nodded, so they got ready to go back to the airport.

As they left, Rocco asked them to follow him over to the Rutan's table. As he approached, he asked Burt if it would be alright if one of them took a picture of the pilots standing behind Dick and Burt. Burt nodded and smiled, so they took turns taking pictures. Rocco told Burt that his crew were ferry pilots just picking up a couple of planes.

Rocco thanked Burt and the other guys and he and his crew went back out into the baking heat of Mojave.

Chapter 52

Lero was waiting in the Pilot's Lounge of the Fixed Base Operator when the pilots and engineers came in. He introduced himself to them and told them he had rooms for them at the Hotel Maggiori and two taxis were waiting.

The rooms at the Hotel were really nice and Lero had arranged for a private dining room so they could have dinner together. They asked him about his flying experiences and he told them about his Air Force service and his time with Braniff Airlines. The pilots and engineers had a lot in common and had a pleasant dinner reviewing their flight from Mojave over the Atlantic and to Geneva. Surprisingly, none of them had been to Geneva before.

After dinner, he told them that the first leg of the tour would leave from Geneva early the next afternoon, so each man could get a good night's rest and a good breakfast in the nice dining room of the Hotel Maggiori before they left.

The next morning, late, he went to the front desk and settled the bill while the pilots and engineers gathered in the lobby with their luggage. He had arranged taxis to take them back to the airport, so no time was lost. At the airport, in the pilot's lounge, he told them that the first leg of the tour would take them to Ovda Airport in Israel, although he left out that it was really Ovda Air Base, and not a civilian airport. Flight plans and the approach plate for Ovda were distributed. Lero had arranged for the planes to be fueled, so the pilots and engineers went out and did their walk arounds and on board checks and got ready to go.

"Geneva ground, this is Lockheed November six one four four bravo, at the fixed base operator's tarmac, ready to taxi in ten minutes, with information Kilo, flight plan on file."

After a brief pause, "Lockheed November six one four four bravo, call when ready to taxi, call clearance delivery now on one two six decimal six, please."

"Clearance, this is Lockheed November six one four four bravo."

"Go ahead, four four bravo. This is Geneva clearance delivery."

"Four four bravo wishes to open flight plan on file, ready to taxi."

"Four four bravo, you are cleared as filed. Expect flight level two four zero ten after departure, squawk three one three one on departure, tower frequency is one one eight decimal five."

"Roger, Clearance, four four bravo back to ground."

By this time the flight engineer had the engines running the the pilots had tuned each radio to the proper communication or navigation frequency. The huge, but empty, L-1011 hummed with activity.

"Ground, four four bravo is ready to taxi."

"Roger, four four bravo. Taxi to runway one six, use taxiway delta. Hold short for landing traffic."

"Roger, four four bravo to runway one six, taxiway delta, hold short."

The hold short line was not at the threshold of the runway. It was set back about two hundred yards, since the active runway was using the glide slope and localizer of the instrument approach system, a large aircraft like the L-1011 would interfere with the transmissions of the glide slope and localizer if it taxied closer to the threshold.

Lero was behind the pilots in the jump seat usually used by non-flying pilots being given a ride to pick up their flights.

"Tower, four four bravo is ready to go on runway one six, holding short."

"Roger, four four bravo, continue to hold short for landing traffic."

"Roger, four four bravo is holding short."

They watched as a graceful Boeing seven forty seven with a Lufthansa paint scheme approached and landed. The tower called again: "Four four bravo, you are cleared onto the runway and cleared for takeoff."

"Roger, tower, four four bravo is rolling."

Just as they pushed the throttles forward, the tower called with a warning.

"Four four bravo, you have a fire in number two engine.

Ogle pulled off the throttles and they aborted the take off.

When the throttle was reduced, the flames ceased.

They taxied back to the tarmac and shut down.

An inspection revealed a loose fuel line fitting and there was no damage to the cowling except some blackened areas, but just as a precaution, they had the maintenance people put in a new fuel line. It took three hours to fabricate the line and install it, while Ogle and Lero waited.

With the fuel line repaired, the crew tried once again to get under way. After the usual calls to ground, clearance delivery and tower, the L-1011 taxied into position at the threshold of Runway 24 at Geneva.

"Pre flight check list complete, ready to roll. Any squawks?" asked Ogle, the pilot in command for this leg.

Non-flying pilot Murphy replied, "No, good to go."

With that reply, Ogle keyed the mike. "Tower, Lockheed four four niner six romeo is ready to go on two four."

"Roger, niner six romeo, clear to take off."

The L0-1011 rumbled into position on the runway and together, Ogle and Murphy brought the thrust levers up to full power. One could hear and feel the tar strips in the old runway as the plane accelerated. In fact, the decreasing times between thumps were good clues to the acceleration of the plane. At one hundred knots, Murphy called, "Vee One." Both pilots glanced again at the airspeed indicators. Shortly after V-One, Murphy called, "Vee R." This was rotation speed and Ogle eased back on the yoke. The liner pitched up and in a couple of seconds, the main landing gear left the runway. Now, both pilots were focusing on the artificial horizon to set the proper pitch up for climb out. When Ogle noticed the vertical speed indicator showed a positive rate of climb, he called, "Gear up." Murphy moved the handle on the panel with the small wheel on the end upward and the plane began to rotate its landing gear into the wells.

"Niner six romeo, begin left turn, climb to four thousand, contact departure control on one two four decimal seven. Good day."

"Roger, Niner six romeo turning left to one seven five, up to four thousand and over to departure. Good day."

By now the plane was high enough to have a perspective of the huge mountains that surround Geneva. Ogle adjusted the heading to pass between two of the peaks as the airliner continued to climb. It passed through between the peaks almost high enough to have cleared them. There were more mountains ahead as far as they could see at that altitude.

"Lockheed niner six romeo, Geneva departure. Cleared to flight level two four zero, maintain one seven zero and squawk three two seven five, please."

"Roger, Departure, niner six romeo cleared up to two four zero, still on one seven zero, squawking three two seven five."

"Niner six romeo, Departure shows your present altitude as one zero, ten thousand feet."

"Roger, departure, niner six romeo is now at ten thousand eight hundred."

"Niner six romeo, join J 43 (an instrument flight high level route) and proceed as filed, Contact Rome center on one three three decimal four five, good day."

Now they were really on their way. All gauges were reading normally and the rate of climb was steady at eleven hundred feet per minute.

They climbed through a thin broken layer of clouds at flight level two seven zero and it was clear above.

In the jump seat, behind the pilots, Lero remembered how it felt to pilot a "ten eleven" in his earlier years as an airline pilot. He wondered how Jean was doing. If her schedule was true to fact, she would be on her way to Aviano today to meet up with the crew of the Poseidon and brief the pilots on the plan.

All three of them in the flight deck watched as the east Italian coast passed by. The blue Adriatic only enhanced the sunlit view below.

"Four Six Romeo, contact South Med center now on one three four decimal one five. Good day."

"Roger, Rome center, four six Romeo over to South Med Center. Good day."

"South Med Center, South Med Center, Lockheed four four six Romeo, level at flight level three one zero."

"Lockheed four six romeo, South Med Center. Continue on your heading of one seven zero and squawk three one zero seven for us please."

"Three one zero seven for four six romeo."

"Radar contact, four six romeo, three hundred ten nautical north west of Ovda."

"Roger, four six romeo."

After a quiet twenty minutes, the earpieces on their radios transmitted, "Four six Romeo, contact Ovda Approach now on one one eight decimal seven five."

"Roger, South Med, four six romeo over to one one eight decimal seven five. Thanks. Good day."

"Ovda Approach, Lockheed four four six Romeo, level at three one zero."

"Four six Romeo, squawk seven one one one for us please."

Murphy tuned the transponder to those numbers and shortly came the response. "Four Six Romeo, radar contact. Descend now to flight level two four zero and report reaching."

"Four six romeo down to two four zero, will report."

Chapter 53

The telephone in the office of the Chief of Staff of the Israeli Defense Forces rang. "General Haim's office, answered Private Helia Gonn.

"This is Lieutenant Bergen in the Ovda Airport tower. General Haim asked to be advised when his friends were approaching. Tell him about twenty minutes."

"Will do, Lieutenant. Thanks," she replied.

She walked to the door of General Haim's office. The General was reviewing written reports from his field commanders and looked up as Private Gonn tapped on the door frame.

"Sir, you asked to be advised when your friends were approaching. Lieutenant Bergen in the tower says about twenty minutes."

"Thank you, Helia," he replied and promptly tossed his pen onto the top of the report he was reading and started for the door. "Please put that report back in its file for me and secure my office. I will take my friends to mess and then the Secure Facility. Call me if you need me."

"Will do, sir," she said and moved out of his way.

In ten minutes, General Haim waited in his Buick at the flight line fence. He got out into the scorching desert heat and stood to watch the approaching flight land. As varied as the aircraft types were that landed at Ovda, it was an unusual event for a large airliner to land there. Ovda was the southern air base of the Israeli Defense Forces. Over one hundred aircraft were based there, including a couple of bombers, but nothing approaching the size of the aircraft that appeared now through the heat ripples about four miles out on approach. He watched as the landing gear came down and the flaps were deployed, remembering his years as an active pilot. The cross wind quickly dispersed the cloud of blue smoke from the main landing gear tires of the L-1011 and it slowed as it approached the turn off to taxi in. A lineman stood with batons to direct the airliner to a parking spot. With the huge nose of the 1011 looming fifty feet from him, the lineman crossed his arms with the batons and the big airliner came to a stop and began shutting down. The ten foot wide air intakes of the engines dwarfed the other linemen as they scuttled about putting chocks in front and behind a couple of tires on each side.

The ground crew pulled up a mobile stairway to the cabin door and, after it opened and was secured, they crew moved the stairway forward until its rubber bumpers touched the skin of the airliner. When the ground crewman gave the waiting crew a thumbs up. They came down the stairway to greet General Haim. Lero let the group and warmly greeted his friend General Tori Haim. They hugged and then Lero introduced Ogle and Murphy to General Haim.

"I imagine you men are hungry after flying all that distance. How about joining me for a little dinner at the mess?"

All three men nodded and smiled. They piled into General Haim's Buick, grateful for the air conditioned relief from the desert heat. A second car stopped behind the Buick and men loaded the gear of the pilots into it.

As they ate dinner in the private dining room, the General briefed the three on the latest intel from the area. Things were pretty quiet on the Sinai border and in that direction, but the Syrian border was a serious concern. Cross border strikes by Hezbollah paid mercenaries were almost a daily occurrence, necessitating a constant vigilance and responsive military actions. The Jordanian border was quiet, with an occasional Palestinian terrorist attack on border outposts.

'We are quite concerned about the situation in Syria. We have refugees piled up at the Syrian border seeking entry. We vet as many as we can who have papers and send them to internment camps just inside our territory. Your government has been very generous with tents, supplies, portable shower houses, food supplies and medical personnel, but we are simply overwhelmed with the numbers. We help from our side of the border, but the major burden of care for the refugees in southern Syria is responded to by your government, some from the United Nations, the Saudi government, France, Italy and Great Britain, but there over four million people displaced. The load is tremendous and, in the meantime, these people are disabled from providing for themselves and going about their productive activities. Most left everything behind to flee."

"Your other crew arrived about three hours ago. We have their aircraft in the large hangar and your men are waiting for us at the Briefing Center. Let's go join them," he said as they finished their meals.

Chapter 54

The one story light brown brick structure bore a sign in the front yard. "Operations Headquarters, Southern Division, IDF."

As they entered, General Haim led the way. The guards at the entry hall immediately recognized him. He turned to Lero and Ogle and Murphy. "Gentlemen, kindly give your IDs to the security personnel. They will scan them and return them." Then, turning to the guards, he said, "These gentlemen are with me. Log them in as Lero, Ogle and Murphy. We will be in my offices."

"Yes, sir," said the shorter, but older guard, and turned to scan the IDs.

Once the head guard indicated that they were cleared to enter, General Haim led them down the central hall. He stopped at the elevator. Ogle and Murphy exchanged glances because they had noticed that the building was a single floor. They all entered the elevator and General Haim inserted a key into the control and rotated it clockwise. The elevator hummed as it descended. The descent went on for several seconds, long enough to descend several floors. When the door opened, they were at a wide hallway.

They followed General Haim to the right down the hallway to a room with only the number sixteen on it. He took out a key and let them in. The first room inside was a waiting room with comfortable chairs. The other pilots and the engineer were waiting for them and immediately rose to greet them. Lero introduced the second crew of pilots and engineer to General Haim. Shortly after they entered, another group of six men entered.

Lero asked Bonham, one of the pilots of the second 1011 if they had any problems along the way. Bonham reported a smooth flight with no squawks.

General Haim, said, "Gentlemen, if you will follow me, please," and led them to the door at the rear of the room. Inside was a nicely appointed briefing room, with flat screen TVs and computer terminals and a large conference table in the middle with comfortable chairs. General Haim motioned them to have a seat.

Once they were all seated and comfortable, General Haim rose to speak. "Gentlemen, I am General Tori Haim, of the Isreaeli Defense Forces. We are involved in this venture, as will be explained to you shortly. The briefing tonight will be given by my friend Lero. Lero is the chief of a small unit of the United States government assigned to special projects. I have known Lero for several years, and without intending to embarrass him, I would say that he is brave and true and has put his life on the line for my country and yours on several occasions. We meet at high purpose tonight, gentlemen. The safety of many people depend on the successful execution of the mission which has been planned and actuated for some weeks now. I will let my friend, Lero, give you the briefing."

Lero thanked General Haim and stood near the end of the table.
"First of all, we want to thank you, General Haim for your warm hospitality. You gents don't know it, but General Haim is a long-time friend of mine and the United States. You are in the briefing center of the Southern Command of the Israeli Defense Forces and General Haim is Chief of Staff of the IDF." He paused to let that sink in.

"Secondly, I want to thank each of you for ferrying these two aircraft to us here." He took a step to more directly face the pilots and engineers, and said, "Then I need to tell you that I am not a tour organizer. I have a more highly placed employer and we are not going to use these aircraft for a tour of dignitaries. Also, Trevette is not my real name, either. You probably heard General Haim call me "Lero." This is my nomme de guerre, or war name. I regret having to deceive you, but we needed civilian pilots with currency in the Lockheed ten eleven and you were chosen for your experience and the fact that, because you were on furlough, you might be available to us. I work for a government contractor based in the western United States. I am going to outline our plan to you, which I must confess, contains some risk. You have been paid the agreed amounts to get you this far, but if you agree to participate with us in this venture, you will each be paid a generous bonus to compensate you for the enhanced risk involved. If any or all of you choose to decline to participate, you will still be paid the agreed remaining balance of the contract price and you will be our guests here for the next few days as we complete our venture."

"If any of you has a cell phone, please put it on the table and turn them off. They will be returned to you later." With a nod from General Haim, a corpsman from the rear of the room collected the cell phones in a basket.

Lero went over and pulled down a roll down chart, showing the area between the Sinai, Cyprus, Syria, the lower part of Turkey, Lebanon, Israel, Jordan, the north eastern portion of Iraq and small portion of Iran.

"Basically, what we plan to do is fly these two aircraft to an airport or airports in Syria to evacuate some sensitive personnel. These people are Syrian nationals with political connections in the opposition to Bashar Assad, church missionaries from various countries, and their spouses and children, volunteer medical personnel, some wounded personnel, special operations people from our respective countries, and others who are trapped in the war zone. There will be enough people to fill both planes to capacity."

"Our personnel will communicate with Syrian air traffic control by way of a recorded fake message to give clearance to the two aircraft, saying that they are delivering ammunition and supplies to Syrian forces. However, we plan to have the planes land at an airport or airports that are, in fact, not controlled by Syrian forces. The refugees, for want of a better word, will be waiting and will board very quickly. You will not even shut down. Once loaded, you will depart on a pre-planned route. Offshore U.S. military aircraft will be jamming all the VHF and UHF frequencies known to be used by the Syrian government. Escort aircraft wlll be waiting just outside of Syrian territory and can come to your rescue if you are jumped by an unexpected fighter."

"I expect that you all know by now that that Malaysian Airliner flying from Amsterdam to Kuala Lumpur was downed over the war zone in Ukraine by a missile fired by Russian controlled forces. We have determined that the missile in question was a Russian Buk missile. Contrary to the usual explosive warhead of surface to air missiles, the Buk carries a charge surrounded by many shaped hardened metal missiles that disburse much like a shrapnel shell when the missile detonates close to the target aircraft. Rather than designed to strike the target and detonate its onboard explosive charge, this missile is designed to shower its target with these metal missiles which will pierce the fuselage of the target, much like the flak first used in the second World War, causing a catastrophic decompression, and usually fracturing the fuselage into parts. The metal particles will kill any personnel unfortunate enough to be struck. Because of the threat of fuselage compromise, we have decided to fly at levels that require minimal pressurization, below twelve thousand feet and at maximum speed, until clear of Syrian airspace. We may have you fly the refugees to Aviano airbase in Italy, or back here, or perhaps to Incirlik, Turkey. This will be decided based on circumstances at the time. Overall command of the air operation will be handled from a U.S. Navy Poseidon aircraft, off shore over the Med. With the speed your aircraft are capable of, we anticipate that the period of enhanced risk will be from twenty to forty minutes, in and out, depending on the airport or airports chosen and the escape route."

"I know this is a lot to dump on you like this. General Haim and I will answer questions and then step out to let you all discuss this among yourselves. When you are ready for us to return, simply knock on the door."

After the group had discussed the mission, sometimes rather loudly, one of them knocked on the door and General Haim and Lero were invited back in.

Captain Rocco was the first to speak. "Well, this comes as substantial surprise. All of us are familiar with the fact that a war is raging in Syria and we also know about the Russian shoot down of the Indonesian Airlines plane over Ukraine. These people you intend to exfiltrate must be very important. Can you tell us more?"

Lero responded, "Each of the intended passengers is loyal to the United States or to Israel or Jordan or is a member or a family member of the opposition to Bashar Assad. Because of the danger to each of these people if they stay in Syria, we decided to try this mechanism to get a large group out. Once we pull this trick, it is very probable that no one could do it again.

Captain Ogle spoke up. "I don't think I can do this. My wife is very ill and will need surgery in the near future. If I did not have that responsibility, I would go, but since she needs me so much right now, I must decline."

The other three pilots and the engineers agreed to go. The extra money offered was very persuasive and they thought it was a fitting use of their skills.

Since they had all pretty much said their pieces, it was now necessary to find another pilot.

General Haim said, "I will ask if we have any qualified and current pilots on this base, but I have serious doubts."

"What do you think, my friend?" he asked, looking at Lero.

Without hesitation, Lero said, "If we cannot find another pilot, I will go." There was a significant silence.

Then, General Haim said, "Lero, my friend, I would not have put you in a position of risk. You are very valuable to our friend, Mr. Murfree. I doubt if he would agree to let you go, but I will not tell him if that is your wish."

"Time is short, General. We need to train and prepare. Look for another pilot, but I will train with the men and will go if you do not find another."

General Haim nodded, and said, "Bring everyone in the mission in here at thirteen hundred hours for the final briefing."

"Alright," said Lero and they rose to leave to get on with it.

Chapter 55

At the appointed time, the men gathered again in the briefing room.

Lero sat at the head of the table. He said, "Alright, fellows, here is the plan. We will depart Ovda late this evening. Time not set yet. Fly over Jordan and then along the Iraq desert to a waypoint near the Iran border. They turn northwest to another waypoint in eastern Syria, then westerly to Aliya airport. Land in tandem, stop at east end of runway, keep engines running. Ladders will be provided by ground personnel. The passengers have been told to board quickly and sort things out later. All of our prospective passengers are to be within a half hour's walk to the west end of the runway. We have arranged for a squad of military personnel to be on hand to act as security, but this is a very touchy project. You must land without landing lights, using night vision goggles. For those of you not familiar with those, there will be an officer here shortly to give each of you sufficient training to put you at ease about using them. You will be given a last minute signal that all is clear to land from an infrared flasher at the east end of the runway. You will receive an approach clearance from the Poseidon. Once you land, turn off runway onto the turn around apron at the west end of the runway and return to the threshold. The passengers will be boarding with ladders furnished by the military squad. They have been told to expedite the boarding and to facilitate the entry of every passenger without delay. Once the ground loadmaster signals to the pilots that all are on board, the doors will be shut and you will take off immediately. The escape route will be given to us by the Poseidon on a discrete frequency. Haul the mail out of there, heading south and the escape route will be communicated to you then. We may use one or more of several potential exit route, so we will choose one or more at the moment, based on latest intelligence. Land where instructed by the Poseidon. Landing airport may change with the circumstances and both planes may not land at the same airport. Once we get you and the planes and the passengers out of there, we will meet again to plan for the return of the planes and to de-brief everyone.

I have had our cartographers prepare a detail map of the area of the airport and a detail map of the airport itself. The runway is nine and two seven and is nine thousand three hundred feet long. It is asphalt, but is rated for heavy aircraft. In the event that the airplanes cannot depart once they land, you will be escorted by the military detachment to safety and we will arrange your exfiltration later.

These aircraft are both equipped with a TransPac kit, meaning extra fuel capacity for you who might not be familiar. You will depart here with enough fuel to carry out the mission to the airport we plan on and you will have enough fuel left on board for flight to any airport in southern Europe.

The extra gents in your midst tonight are military corpsmen who will see to the medical needs of any of the passengers who are known to be wounded or become injured in the effort to get to the airport and board.

I will remain with you and can answer your questions. General Haim, thank you again for you hospitality and your assistance."

General Haim rose, nodded with a smile and left the briefing room.

Lero signaled to the men present that he wanted to say a bit more.

"I should tell you that General Haim's son, Ari, was killed along with another officer and numerous civilians by two terrorists on a motorcycle with a bomb. They rode directly into the restaurant where Ari and his associate were eating lunch and detonated the device. General Haim and his friends at Mossad have determined that the hit was ordered by Assad himself and the commander of Hezbollah in Syria, so you can see why he is motivated to do everything he can to help Assad's opposition."

One could have heard a pin drop. Then the room gradually resumed normal conversational tones.

Chapter 56

Amal watched the opening intently. It was his turn to guard the opening. It was what was left of a hallway in the basement of their three story apartment building. He and the others were hiding in what was left of the basement. Assad's partisans were all around, night and day. They huddled as quietly as they could when the troops were nearby. They only wandered out to look for food and water at night. Only a couple of the adults went out. The children had been inside for nine days now.

Amal clutched the AK-47 and leaned on it. He was sleepy, but needed to stay awake until he was relieved. If a soldier discovered them and started into the opening, about thirty feet from where he hid, he would probably have to shoot. If they were discovered, it would mean death for them all, for they were aligned with the resistance. The neighborhood around them in Aliya was decimated. Most of the buildings were either destroyed or weakened by howitzer rounds that they were in danger of collapsing. The eleven of them had been hiding in the remnant of the basement of the apartment building for more than three weeks, hoping for rescue, but becoming more discouraged as each day passed without any contact.

As he watched, the feet and ankles of a man appeared near the upper left corner of his field of view out the opening. The man was using a walking stick to steady himself in the rubble of the building. Amal noticed that the lower third of the stick was wrapped with a red and white cloth. It was the insignia of his secret group of resistance fighters. All were scattered now, some had fled to Jordan, some were in camps near the south border, some had been captured and shot and others were hiding out like him, hoping for a chance to get out of the war zone and have a life.

The stick stopped near the opening. It was dusk and but Amal could see the red and white wrapping on the stick clearly. The man stood there for several minutes. Then, he stooped and looked into the opening. Amal recognized him immediately. It was Yosuf, his neighbor. Yosuf had lived in the next door building which was now only a pile of rubble. Yosuf had fled with his family earlier in the conflict, when it was easier to slip through the loyalist lines and get out of the war zone. Yosuf peered into the opening and called in a hoarse and quiet whisper. "Any body there?"

Amal quickly whispered back. "Yes, Yosuf. Come in quickly."

Yosuf crawled into the opening and made his way back to where Amal was standing guard.

The two men hugged like comrades do when they have faced danger and found each other after a long struggle.

"How many are you?" asked Yosuf, after they finished greeting each other.

"There are eleven of us. Sami and Kamil and their wives and children, and my wife and our two children. We have had no food for three days now. Water is about used up, too. The shelling is terrible, but the loyalists have about destroyed all the buildings and only shell intermittently now."

"I brought you some food and water," said Yosuf and he opened his back pack and gave Amal the food and bottles of water.

Amal, asked, "Will you guard while I crawl back and give the food and water to the others?"

Yosuf nodded and took the rifle to stand watch.

In a few minutes, Amal returned and Yosuf handed him the rifle back.

"I have news, Amal," said Yosuf.

He handed Amal a paper map with markings on it.

"Tomorrow night at one AM, I need you and your others to be at the spot marked on the map. Bring what you can carry. Nothing more. We are being rescued. There will be several groups. I cannot tell you more, but be ready to leave Syria for a while. Each of my group will have two or three families to organize. Say nothing to anyone other than your group here. We cannot know who is loyal to us or to Assad. The place for you to hide and wait is a bombed out building that will be marked with a yellow splash of paint on the north side. Hide inside until I come for you. It is a long walk at night for your group. Seventeen kilometers. There is danger, but we have chosen a route that has the best probability of escape without detection. If you are about to be captured, tear the map into tiny parts and swallow it or destroy it with fire. The map will allow the partisans to locate and kill the whole group if it is captured."

"I understand," said Amal. "We are very grateful. I hope someday to be able to repay you for this kindness, Yosuf."

"If we get to die as old men in a free Syria, it will be thanks enough, my friend," Yosuf said.

They shook hands warmly.

Yosuf said, "See you tomorrow night." He turned and crawled back out the tunnel. In a minute, he was gone. Amal stayed at his position until the end of his shift, wondering what kind of a rescue was planned.

Josuf visited three other groups that night.

Chapter 57

The radio speaker in the bunker of the Fifth Division of the loyalist Syrian Army crackled to life. The attending communications officer and the others huddled in the communications office all looked at the speaker, as if looking at it would enhance the clarity of the message, if any. The radio was scanning a pre-set group of frequencies and this was the security frequency for this sector of the theatre of battle.

"(In Arabic.) Attention. Attention. This is General Assoud. Our brothers in the Islamic Republic are going to favor us with a pair of aircraft transporting ammunition and food and medical supplies tonight. The two aircraft will land at two different airports near the south of Aleppo. For security purposes, I am directing that no one is to fire at any aircraft between the hours of midnight and three AM tonight. These are large transport aircraft and pose no threat to our troops. We are most grateful to our brothers in this struggle for their assistance. May Allah save Syria. That isall."

The officer and men hesitated only a moment before beginning to disseminate the information. Within an hour, every man they could reach knew the plan. Sporadic gunfire continued in the night and occasional flashes of shell bursts lit the evening. Compared to recent activity, it was a relatively quiet night, though.

At flight level four one zero, the Posiedon hissed through the sky above the Mediterranean Sea. Jean took the thumb drive with the recorded message from General Assoub from the port in the computer and put it in the drawer to her left. She continue to monitor the frequency and wondered where Lero and his men were and what they were doing. It was ominously quiet.

In the dark, Lieutenant Siegermann felt for the loose brick in the damaged wall. He found it and removed it carefully. Behind it was a small plastic container, the type used for thirty five millimeter film. He quickly grabbed it and replaced the brick, then scurried away from the drop to a place to hide and check his return route, as far as he could see in the dark, before he returned to the hide. Forty minutes later, after evading two Syrian Army patrols, he tapped quietly on the door of the partially destroyed school where he and his squad had hidden. The other three looked at him in anticipation of any news.

"It is quieter tonight. Still dangerous. I saw two patrols. We could use the suppressed weapons to snipe at loyalist patrols if we choose, but I think it better that we hide here tonight and get some rest. I will decode the message and share it with you," he whispered. The others nodded agreement and they waited as he took out the code book that Myron had in his backpack. Myron was the designated custodian of the code book. He kept it next to the thermite grenade in his backpack. If he set off the thermite grenade, the codebook would be one of the first things destroyed.

The numbers in neat rows decoded to a cryptic message: "Exfil 9/16 at 2 AM local. Be at bombed out school 34 12 14.5 N 25 20 33.6 E for contact. Contact will use infrared flashlight. Four short flashes. Return three. Good luck."

He showed the handwritten decoded message to the three others. They expressed pleasure without speaking. Then all four of them tried to get some sleep. It was difficult, however, with all the stress over shelling and the thoughts of going home to their loved ones tomorrow.

As Amal and his wife, Katryn, carried their youngsters through the night and through the rubble of their bombed out village, they came upon a stretch of rubble that they had to cross in order to avoid discovery by the partisans at the observation point in the second floor window of the partially destroyed apartment building across the street. The street was strewn with boulder sized fragments of concrete walls and debris. As they sneaked along, at a moment of silence, Amal stepped on a soft spot and his leg went into the crevice between pieces of blocks. There was a ominous "crack." Amal grimaced in pain and collapsed with his son in his arms. Katryn came back to him. Amal was able to tell her that he had broken his leg above the right ankle. He was in such pain that he could not get up, let alone walk any farther. He begged Katryn to take the other child and go ahead to the place where they were to wait for Yosuf to come and take them the next part of their journey. They wept as Amal handed her the strap from the canteen, the only water they had. She hugged his neck and kissed him. He said he would find his way alone or with help, but that she must go ahead with the children. Baby Jesse was asleep in the blanket that Katryn had wrapped around them both. She hung in front of her mother in the blanket. Their son, Kori, watched with big brown eyes as his parents parted and he was taken on his way by the hand of his mother into the night. He looked back, heartbroken, as he left his father with his mother.

Chapter 58

Now that they were down to three pilots and Lero was filling in to make a fourth, the men began their final preparations for the flight. General Haim met with them in the briefing room and gave them their flight charts for the evening.

"Your man Jefe and Jean are the only other people who know the actual destination of your flight tonight," he said. "There is no need to share that information with anyone. Once you are airborne on the way out, we can provide you guidance away from any known threats by secure air traffic advisories from the Poseidon. Where you will land after the flight out will be decided based on what diversions you need to make on the way. We will have appropriate personnel ready to await your arrival with your passengers at six different airports."

"Lero, do you have any advice for these gentlemen?" asked General Haim.

"First of all, I want to thank each of you for undertaking this mission. There is some danger to us, our aircraft and our passengers. My general advice would be to stay low so as to traverse the field of vision of people on the ground quickly, conserve fuel going in. These aircraft have plenty of speed, so we can take it easy going in. Coming out, I would also advise you to stay relatively low and use all available speed. Once we are clear of hostile airspace, we can resume normal flight operations. General, where are we going tonight?" he asked of General Haim.

General Haim spoke slowly and clearly, looking at them in turn around the table, "Your destination in Syria is a remote field south of the town of Aliya. These charts show the airport and the navigation aids near it. Some of them will probably not be working, so you must make a visual approach. Our people in the Poseidon will provide guidance. It is a former military base, now used occasionally for commercial flights, but due to the hostilities, it is pretty much deserted. Our people will cruise the runway for debris and damage as soon as you take off and will maintain eyes on until you arrive. As you make your final approach, if you see a red flare over the runway, abort the mission and make for the Syrian border to the southwest. Because of secrecy, the runway will be designated and lit marginally by vehicles parked at the east and west ends of the runway, which is niner and two seven. As soon as you land, turn off the landing lights and all external lights as soon as it is safe to do so. When you stop at the west end of the runway, friendly forces will provide ladders for the people to board. They have been told to expedite boarding and to sort seat arrangements later. It is anticipated that you will be on the ground less than fifteen minutes. Park where you see the man with the green flashlight as you taxi up. Do not shut down the engines. Depart to the east and turn to the south as soon as practical. Your exit routes will be given to you by the Poseidon. A loadmaster on the ground will signal you with a green flashlight, several long flashes when you are cleared to depart. There is a wide apron at the west end of the runway at Aliya, so you can turn around there."

Lero said, "There is a list of frequencies on your charts. We will be using unused frequencies for the area, so that we can communicate as well as possible. If you suspect that you are being talked to my someone other than one of the four of us, say the words 'Tally Ho,' and all of us will know to try another frequency. So as not to give any clue as to the number of aircraft in our flight, we will use the call signs, "Blue Bird' and 'Red Bird.' Rocco and I and Everson will be Red Bird."

After General Haim completed his briefing, he stood and said, "Gentlemen, thank you again for undertaking this mission. You will always have a friend in me for doing this. The people you will save will be able to sit out this war in safety and, in the case of the military personnel, will be able to return safely to their families after a long period behind enemy lines."

He turned and walked from the room. Lero said, "The General is too humble to tell you that one of the commandos behind enemy lines that we will ex-filtrate tonight is his grandson, Levi. You are definitely doing a good thing tonight, men."

He then reviewed the flight plan with them. They would depart Ovda and fly east across into Jordan and Iraq to a waypoint south of the Syrian border in Iraq, thirty four degrees thirty seconds, zero minutes North, forty two degrees zero minutes zero seconds East, then north to a point thirty six degrees north zero minutes zero seconds North, Forty two degrees zero minutes zero seconds East, just east of the Syrian border with Iraq, in line with the northern part of Iran. Then they would turn northwesterly and cross into Syria. They would land at Aliya south of Aleppo at approximately one AM, local time, load quickly and take off to the east with an immediate turn to the southwest and fly low and fast to the Syrian border with Lebanon and then out over the Mediterranean.

Working together, they designed a GPS approach to the landing airport. Ten miles out they established a waypoint and decided, based on the altitude of the field, to be at eighteen hundred feet MSL over that waypoint. They established another waypoint two miles from the field and decided to be at twelve hundred feet MSL over that waypoint. From there, they would make their landing using the headlights of the vehicles at the threshold and the far end of the runway. The plan was that as soon as the planes landed, the lights would be turned off. When they were to take off, once safely outside of Syrian airspace, they would fly to Ovda by circling south along the Israeli coast and then inland to the airport. The alternates for landing were Aviano in Italy, Incirlik in Turkey, and Nicosia, Cyprus. They syncronized their watches and gathered up their duffels and gear and walked out to the elevator. Once back up on ground level, a pair of vans waited for them outside and they boarded for the short drive to the flight line.

Chapter 59

Seventeen kilometers is about ten miles. A normal adult, walking without impediments, can walk about four miles an hour. With her child asleep in the sling across her front and her young son on her left hand, Katryn, struggled. The terrain was intermittently clear and easy to walk, and sometimes strewn with the debris of bombed out buildings and military hardware. In three hours she had made it more than half way. She worried constantly about Amal. With a broken leg, in hostile territory, unarmed, frightened and with no means of communication, he was in dire straits. She wondered if she would ever see him again. He had been such a good husband. He was shy and tender and bookish. He had worked as a clerk at a bank in their village and would probably someday be a banker if peace ever came. Now, he lay wounded in hostile territory. Would he make it to the meeting place to escape with them? Would she ever see him again? She wept as she trudged along in the dark. Her young son sensed the terror of the situation and kept unusually silent. She was grateful for that, for his sake and hers.

Chapter 60

Amal could hear footsteps in the darkness. The rubble made footing difficult and he could hear the boots crunching along in the gravel created by the bombing of buildings. Exposed as he was, he was a sitting duck if the men were hostile. He leaned forward to make his silhouette a low as possible. When the footsteps got within a few feet, they stopped. He could hear the men whispering. "Look, it is a dead civilian." "Be careful, his body may be booby trapped." "Can you tell if he is a loyalist or a rebel?" One man carefully edged forward. He nudged Amal with his boot. Amal stirred and the men were startled. Throwing caution to the wind, Amal said, in Arabic, "Help me, I have broken my right leg." The men kept their weapons trained on him while one searched him. His broken leg was causing Amal intense pain and they could readily see that he was so overcome with pain that he was no threat to them. Two of the soldiers gathered him up and put his arms over their shoulders and helped him forward. There was a bombed out building about fifty yards forward and they went into a room that had had the wall destroyed and was open to them. The took his sandal off and wrapped his swelling ankle with a bandage.

"Where are you going?" asked the soldier in charge.

"I was going to meet a friend about five kilometers south of here," Amal said.

"We are with the people's militia, fighting against Assad's forces. Which group are you loyal to?" he asked.

"I have a wife and two small children. I could not participate in the fighting. I have no weapon, but our loyalty is with those opposed to Assad," he said.

"Where were you going tonight?" asked the soldier.

"I was going to the village of Mira, to meet a friend to get some food for my family," said Amal.

"What is your friend's name?" asked the soldier.

"Yosuf is his name," said Amal.

The men were startled.

"What is Yosuf's family name," asked the soldier.

"Mansour," said Amal.

The soldier grinned. "You have had good luck. We know Yosuf and we are going to meet him tonight, also. You may come with us, if you want."

Amal smiled and nodded enthusiastically.

Chapter 61

Ovda ground, Red bird at the south tarmac, ready for engine start in ten minutes, flight plan on file, requesting taxi instructions for a departure to the east."

"Roger, Redbird. Ovda weather is ceiling six thousand scattered, visibility twenty miles, wind is eight knots from three zero zero, altimeter setting is two niner niner niner. Runway one six is the active. Report back when ready to taxi."

The flight deck of Redbird was alive. The pilots and engineer went through the pre-flight check list. There were eighty two items.

"Let's set the waypoints together, just to be sure we enter them correctly," said Lero.

Rocco nodded. Lero read the latitude and longitude of waypoint one. They both looked at the display and agreed that it was correctly displayed. Lero pushed the button to confirm its entry. They they input the latitude and longitude for waypoint two, just east of the Syrian border in Iraq. Then they carefully input the waypoint for the ten mile out landing approach and the two mile out approach waypoint. At ten miles out, they planned to be at two thousand feet MSL and at the two miles out waypoint, they planned to be at twelve hundred feet MSL, only three hundred feet above the airport elevation. They had agreed on a rate of descent at the ten miles out waypoint to descent to the two miles out waypoint "on altitude." When they had agreed to the waypoint's coordinates on the display, Lero pushed the "Enter" button again. Now all they had to do after takeoff was engage the autopilot and instruct it to fly the plane to waypoint one. Once there, they would instruct the autopilot to fly the plane to waypoint two. The flight to the approach waypoints would then be chosen on the autopilot. When all the challenges and responses had been called and responded to, they were ready to start the engines. The pilots and engineer nodded to each other indicating that they were ready for engine start. Rocco, the pilot flying for takeoff, instructed Lero to start engine number one.

"Number one turning," responded Lero as he held the start button down and watched the gauges to see the revolutions come up. When the revolutions reached six thousand, the power indicator jumped to life, indicating that the engine was producing power. As the gauges settled, he responded to Rocco, "Engine number one running and normal."

As soon as Lero had all three engines running, Rocco keyed his headset microphone with the button on the yoke.

"Ovda ground, Redbird is ready to taxi."

"Roger, Redbird. Taxi to runway one six."

"Redbird to runway one six, Roger."

Lero looked back into the passenger compartment of the L-1011. It was huge and empty. Then he turned his attention once again to the panel and his team in the flight deck.

As they taxied, they could hear Bluebird call ground control for permission to taxi. Now the whole team was on the roll.

"Ovda tower, Redbird is ready to go on One Six."

"Redbird, Ovda Tower, cleared for take-off. Godspeed."

"Roger, Tower, Thanks. Redbird rolling."

Rocco and Lero together moved the thrust levers forward. After about four seconds the thrust levers hit the forward stops and the engines were at maximum take-off thrust. The gigantic aircraft surged forward. The clock indicate eleven minutes after ten, local time.

With a full load of fuel, but no passengers or luggage, the L-1011 was lighter than normal and they reached rotation speed quickly. Redbird raised its nose gear on command and they vaulted into the night.

Usually, as soon as an aircraft clears the runway environment, the tower directs the pilot to contact departure control. On this night, the frequency was ominously silent. They were on their own and they knew it. Lero switched the second communications radio, call a "com" by the pilots, to the frequency previously agreed to which would keep them in constant contact with the Poseidon. No one spoke, but the Poseidon was "there" if they needed help. They set a heading of zero seven zero and watched the course deviation indicator swing toward the middle, indicating that they were on course to waypoint one.

They heard Bluebird ask for and receive take-off clearance and announce that they were rolling for take-off on Runway One Six. The frequency resumed its quiet. In the Poseidon, Jean spoke a silent prayer for Lero and his friends. She watched their progress on her radar scope. The two planes showed up as primary returns since they were not using their transponders. The next three hours or so would be very tense. She knew that the military leaders of U. S. Forces in Iraq had briefed those who needed to know about the flights into Iraqi airspace. She expected to hear nothing from them on their discrete frequency unless there was a problem.

Chapter 62

Lieutenant Siegermann and his squad trudged through the night and the rubble, with Amal still being supported by the shoulders of two of his men. They switched off periodically to let the carriers rest. Amal was in a lot of pain from the leg fracture, so they gave him a styrette of morphine. That alleviated most of the pain, but it made him less able to cling to them for support. By eleven PM local time, they still had five kilometers to go, by their reckoning. They had to stop periodically to avoid detection by roving patrols of partisans and Syrian soldiers. Luckily, it was a dark night, with no moon and a high overcast. If one could have visualized it, one would have seen hundreds of people converging on the Aliya airport. Some in cars, some in donkey drawn wagons, most on foot. All were carrying their dearest possessions and some food. Some were carrying children and some were carrying the sick or wounded. The desert was alive with souls, but, they all gave a strong effort to remain out of sight. Each team leader had been instructed to halt his group's approach at a designated spot and await the signal to hurry onto the airport. It was nearing midnight. All was quiet.

Chapter 63

Lero and Rocco in Redbird were nearing waypoint one. They were holding speed to two hundred knots and altitude at twelve thousand. At that altitude, they were gulping fuel at twice the rate as they would have been at flight level three one zero or above, but they had plenty of fuel since these airplanes both had TransPac modifications with huge fuel tanks for airline service across the Pacific Ocean. They kept the airplanes below the altitudes at which they would need oxygen and where the pressurization would be minimal in case the fuselage or fuel tanks would be pierced by ground fire. They cruised along with no external lights. They monitored the air traffic control frequencies of the sectors of Jordanian airspace and Iraqi airspace through which they traversed, but heard no reference to the two primary returns on air traffic control's radar screens.

"I make it about ten minutes to waypoint one," said Lero to Rocco.

"Okay," said Rocco. We will turn to a heading of three six zero about three minutes before we get to the waypoint to join a three sixty heading from the waypoint toward waypoint two."

"Okay," said Lero in the right seat. "Two minutes now to beginning the turn."

They sat quietly as the L-1011 hissed through the night and then Lero said, "Initiate turn now to three six zero."

"Right," said Rocco and he turned the heading bug on the autopilot to initiate a left turn. When he judged that they had turned enough, he returned the heading bug to three six zero and watched with Lero as the course deviation indicator settled to the middle of its range, indicating that they were on a course of three six zero.

"How long do you make it to waypoint two?" asked Rocco.

"At this speed, approximately thirty eight minutes," said Lero.

"Okay. Give me a heads up every ten minutes or so, please," asked Rocco.

"Will do," said Lero. Both men physically and psychologically sat up more erect in their seats. Things were heating up. Lero watched the GPS unwind in its distance reading to waypoint two. In a few minutes, he spoke, "About twenty five minutes now."

"Roger," said Rocco.

Chapter 64

At the north perimeter fence of Aliya airport, a squad of Israeli Commandos huddled in the underbrush. In keeping with the covert nature of their mission, they were in plain attire, not uniforms. They approached the fence crawling. One soldier took out a pair of clippers from the backpack of his companion and began methodically cutting a large opening in the fence, carefully leaving it connected at the top. The opening was about eight feet wide and just short of six feet tall. The few strands at the top kept the section of fence from parting and collapsing, which would have quickly drawn some attention they did not want. Sergeant Ackor and Corporal Flinders set up a sniper position where they could observe anyone who might approach from inside the fence. The other members of the patrol kept a lookout for persons approaching on the outside of the fence. Ackor had a FAL seven decimal six five millimeter rifle with a suppressor on its muzzle and a night vision telescope sight. The suppressor was so effective that when the rifle fired, the loudest noise the nearby observer would hear would be the bolt closing on the subsequent round. Axkor swept an arc from left to right looking for any motion or person approaching. With the night vision telescope, Ackor was confident that he could hit an object the size of a pie plate within three hundred yards. It was nearing midnight.

Siegermann got out and checked his infrared strobe light to signal the other group leaders where they could enter the fence when the time came. Siegermann noticed that there was activity behind them. He watched through his night vision goggles as the desert scrub terrain was dotted with moving objects, all seemingly moving toward him and his men. He alerted his men with a hand signal and reaffirmed his earlier command to hold fire unless fired upon or his command. He knew that the target time was one AM, but he also knew that things this complicated rarely go off without some shifting of times. Still, he whispered to the nearest of his men so he could pass the word along: "One hour."

Lero spoke softly, "Waypoint two in five minutes."

Rocco just nodded and reached for the heading bug. When Lero said three minutes, Rocco turned the heading bug about ten degrees and the big plane began to turn in the night. There were no lights on the ground. It was like a moonscape, but they expected to see ground lights after they crossed into Syria.

"Coming up on a heading of two six five," said Rocco. "How long to the first approach waypoint?"

"I make it thirty seven minutes," said Lero. The course deviation indicator centered on a setting of two sixty five. They were still at twelve thousand feet, making two hundred knots.

Both men hoped that all the Syrian troops had gotten the bogus message from General Ayoub that they were not to fire on any aircraft during this three hour time band. This was the sweatiest part of the trip. No one spoke.

High above the Mediterranean, Jean watched as the two tiny primary returns crept across her scope toward the heart of Syria.

Chapter 65

Seigermann and his patrol, with Amal being carried, halted about a half kilometer from the perimeter fence and huddle down to await the infrared strobe signal to approach the fence and then sprint for the expected aircraft. No one spoke and had not spoken for more than an hour.

Seigermann could see activity to his left and right, going in the same direction, but his people only watched. The rule was not to fire unless fired upon or ordered to do so. Within a few minutes he could spot several groups of people, all halting at about the same distance from the fence. Seigermann put on his infrared goggles to await the signal.

Chapter 66

Jefe stood next to the radar feed from the Poseidon. He was in the Combat Information Center of the Central Intelligence Agency in Langley, Virginia. By order, there were only three other people in the cubicle where he watched. He had made sure that the same feed was going to General Haim at Ovda. There were people from a dozen known countries, and probably were other countries represented, but the main thrust was to get these endangered people out of Syria. Separately, Haim and Jefe watched the radar as the two blips eased into Syrian airspace and started toward Aliya.

"How long do you calculate to Aliya," he asked Jean on the secure scrambled frequency.

"About thirty three minutes," she said.

"Okay," Jefe said. "I will stay off the frequency. We are watching."

"Roger," was the only reply. The Poseidon was about sixty miles offshore over the Mediterranean at flight level four one zero. The very few people in on the operation were tensed up as the moment approached.

The desert terrain was quiet, but Seigermann and his squad could see movement around them and knew that the people were assembling under the cover of night.

Lero and Rocco had dimmed the flight deck lights so they could see outside better. The landscape sweeping toward them was mostly unlit desert. Occasional small groups of lights would appear and then pass under the nose of the L-1011. The altitude was a compromise. It would enable ground troops to observe them better, but it would not carry the stress of worry about a surface to air missile that, at a high altitude, would cause the aluminum cocoon of the airplane to fracture like an egg if hit. No one had spoken for several minutes, when Lero said, almost in a whisper over the intercom, "Twenty minutes. Course is good. Stand by to decelerate as we approach. Fifty miles to the ten mile landing waypoint. Better start down."

Rocco reached over between them and pulled the thrust levers back a bit. The plane, nosed over a bit in response to the reduction in power. When the descent steadied on eight hundred feet per minute, Rocco reduced power again. Soon, they were at ten thousand feet above Mean Seal Level and about eight thousand feet above the terrain. A large center of population appeared off to the right. Both Rocco and Lero knew that that area encompassed Aleppo and its suburbs. The terrain ahead was dotted with widely separated lights. Both knew that Aliya lay directly ahead.

Lero said, "Passing ten mile waypoint. Begin descent to five thousand MSL."

"Gear down," responded Rocco.

"Gear coming down," said Lero. "V-ref at this weight is one forty knots."

(Vref is the approach speed, which is calculated for the weight of the aircraft, so pilots can compensate for the change in weight as fuel is burned off, but Vref can be raised or lowered due to wind or field conditions.)

"Flaps five," said Rocco and Lero moved the flap lever to the five degree position. They both noticed that the plane decelerated with that event, as it had when they put the gear down.

"Three green lights on the gear," said Lero.

Rocco said, "Roger, three green on the gear."

Altitude now five thousand five hundred. Coming up on five mile waypoint in one decimal eight miles.

"Down to five, speed on one five zero,"said Rocco.

The terrain ahead was black. No lights. As they passed over the five mile waypoint, they began another descent to two thousand feet. Now the airspeed was one forty five. No lights on the plane. Dark night. Tense moment.

"We should see the truck lights any time," said Lero and just as he said it, they appeared.

Rocco made a slight adjustment to the left and pulled off more thrust.

They could both see the ground now. The trucks at the near end of the runway looked big in the windscreens. The big plane swept over the trucks and touched down about five hundred feet farther. As soon as they were securely settled on the main gear, Rocco applied thrust reverse and the nose gear settled to the runway. Speed was now about ninety and they continued to decelerate. They could see the far end of the runway and the turn-around apron off to the right. They continued to decelerate. As soon as they turned off the runway onto the apron, the truck lights went out. It was black dark again. Lero and Enderson, the engineer, left their seats and sprinted back to open the passenger doors. As soon as the plane came to a stop, they opened the doors. They had not had a chance to suspect that they whole operation might have been compromised and that enemy soldiers might be waiting for them. Lero threw open his door and immediately a ladder thudded against the threshold.

"Welcome to Aliya, Redbird," came the greeting. Lero heaved a sigh of relief. A second ladder appeared and people began pouring up the ladders. They had been instructed to go as far inside as they could so they could fill the plane quickly.

Lero spotted Anya and her toddlers in the crowd. They did not look particularly distinctive, but her face bore the expression of deep concern, not the jubilation of most of the people flooding onto the L-1011. When she got up the ladder with the child in her arms and her young son clinging to her skirt, Lero asked if he could help her.

"Yes," she said. "My husband fell and broke his leg earlier this evening. I had to leave him behind. I am so grateful to get myself and my children out, but I am so concerned for my husband. I hope he is not captured by the enemy or killed."

"What is his name? I will ask about him," Lero said.

"His name is Amal Mansour. He is thirty six year old. Thank you."

"Get a good seat for yourself and your children. We will be leaving very soon."

Lero looked back over the crowd of people lining up to climb the ladders. The rear door had two ladders up, too, and people were streaming in. As he surveyed the crowd, it looked like more people than they were expecting. As he came to that conclusion, Bluebird taxied to stop about thirty yards behind Redbird. The crowd parted instinctively, it seemed, and a large contingent of the people surged toward Bluebird.

As the rear of the crowd scurrying to get on Redbird became visible, Lero noticed that there was a squad of commandos walking backwards toward them, with their weapons trained on the darkness behind the crowd. They were the rear guard and would be the last to board. As they got closer, he saw that one of the men was being carried by the arms over the shoulders of two of the commandos. They got to the ladder and everyone had boarded but them. Lero got to his knees and helped them lift the injured man up the ladder. Amal used his arms on the ladder to help. When Lero got him into the doorway, he took the man by the shoulders and asked, "Are you Amal Mansour?"

The man was surprised to be called by his name, but nodded "Yes."

"Your family is back there. Welcome aboard."

Two of the commandos helped Amal back to rejoin his family. There was a cheer from the people huddled near his family. One commando patted Amal on the shoulder as Amal settled into a seat. His leg was wrapped in bandages and a fiberglass splint. He was in pain, on the one hand, but overjoyed to be with his family on their way to safety, on the other. He looked up and sobbed. Lero patted him on the shoulder again and turned to get back to the flight deck. As he hustled up the aisle, the commandos were instructing the people to put their seatbelts on, using sign language. The commandos pushed the ladders away and closed the doors.

Lero got back to the flight deck in time for him and Rocco to watch the last of the passengers board Bluebird. It had come to a halt just offset enough from Redbird that Lero and Rocco could see what was happening from the flight deck.

"We need to get out of here," Rocco said to Lero.

"They have pushed the ladders away. We can go," said Lero.

"Roger that," said Rocco and he had one hand on the brake release and the other on the tiller to operate the nose wheel to taxi back onto the runway. Lero glanced at the fuel gauges and was pleased to see that they had more than half full tanks.

"I did not count the people as they boarded, but it looks like the equivalent of about three hundred twenty five, counting the children. Weight will probably be about fifty thousand pounds short of max gross take off weight."

"Okay," said Rocco. Set flaps at five for takeoff."

Lero said, "The ladders are away on Bluebird. We are good to go."

"Roger, Brake release," said Rocco and he turned the nose gear to the left to steer the plane back onto the runway. They did not hesitate at the runway's edge like a normal flight, but Rocco brought the thrust levers up to maximum as the nose gear passed onto the runway. He adjusted a bit to get the plane onto the center of the runway as they accelerated.

V-one is one hundred ten knots," said Lero. He had calculated that based on his estimate of the passenger load.

"V-r is one fifteen," he added.

Rocco, intently watching the airspeed build, just said, "Roger."

Lero and Rocco knew that Bluebird would be wasting no time to get onto the same runway and begin their take off roll, too.

Sweeney had already set take off power in Bluebird and they surged forward about a thousand feet behind Redbird.

"V-one," called Lero. Rocco did not respond.

"V-r," called Lero. Rocco nodded, but did not respond.

Rocco pulled back on his yoke and the nose gear left the runway. Three seconds later, the main gear broke ground and Redbird leaped into the night.

As the altimeter indicated about eight hundred feet above the runway, Rocco nosed the aircraft over and leveled, then initiated a right turn. Lero could see back into the night as they turned, but did not see Bluebird. Both planes were still blacked out. No lights. Rocco leveled off at three thousand feet MSL and kept the power levers at maximum. Their heading was now two four five degrees, southwest.

"Let's go south of Damascus and out over the Med," said Lero.

"Good idea. The thought of all those people in Damascus with weapons is daunting. Is this altitude okay with you?" Rocco asked.

"You bet, the lower the better. I know we are eating up fuel, but we have plenty. In twenty minutes we will out over the Med and we can do as we wish about altitude.

Chapter 67

"Your re-supply mission south of Aleppo is going well, General," said Colonel Hasan, saluting smartly.

General Assoud looked up smartly from the charts on his desk, "What re-supply mission?"

"The one you announced on the discrete military frequency, sir," said Hasan with a proud smile.

"I gave no such announcement or order, Colonel Hasan. What is happening?"

"The two supply planes landed at Aliya about an half an hour ago and just took off ten minutes ago. It would appear that they are headed out toward the Mediterranean."

"There is some kind of treachery afoot, Colonel. I gave no such orders. Shoot the planes down immediately. Send up fighters, too, if it is not too late," said General Assoud.

It only took a couple of minutes for the orders to trickle down to the Buk surface to air missile site on the north side of Damascus. Their radar had picked up the two planes when the planes got within fifty miles.

Major Domotrovich stood behind his radar technician as they surveyed the screen.

"There are the two planes, Major. One is headed for the Mediterranean and almost to the shore. The other is east of us, heading for the Jordanian border."

"How many Huks do we have ready?" asked the Major.

"One on the launcher and three in reserve, Sir," answered the gunnery sergeant.

"The one headed for the Mediterranean is too close to the coast to reach in time. Shoot the other one down immediately," said the Major.

"Yes sir," said the gunnery sergeant and turned his key to arm the weapon. The radar technician input the present position of the plane into the missile's computer and it acknowledged the receipt.

"The missile is ready to go, Sir," said the technician. The gunnery sergeant was listening on the same intercom channel and said, "Ready to go here, sir."

"Very well, launch the missile," said Domotrovich.

Instantly after the radar technician turned his key, there was a bright light and a horrendous noise as the missile left its carrier. The night sky was lit up and anyone within miles would see the flash.

"Missile away, sir. All systems functioning normally," said the radar technician, as they both watch in fascination as the missile on the screen closed with the target.

The first warning that they had been discovered came when ground fire raked the side of the Redbird. There was little damage, but a passenger was struck in the neck and died instantly.

"Fat's in the fire," said Lero and Rocco began to take evasive maneuvers while maintaining a base course toward the Jordanian border.

As they looked out into the dark landscape, they could see the fiery trail of the missile coming toward them. Only a few seconds later, the missile exploded on the pilot's side of the nose of the L-1011. There was a large flash and the explosion of the warhead jarred the entire airplane. A large hole was blown in the side of the flight deck. Rocco was killed by shrapnel and his side of the panel as well as his yoke was blown away. Rocco's body, terribly mangled, lay in what was left of his seat. Lero was struck in the left upper arm by a piece of shrapnel and he was deafened by the blast. Everson, the engineer, was hanging by his seatbelt from his seat behind Lero. Air streamed into the cockpit at two hundred knots. Debris flew through the cockpit for a few seconds, then was blown overboard. The noise was deafening for those who could hear.

Lero did not touch the power levers. They were completely forward and the L-1011 was making over two hundred knots, so he let it ride. He immediately pushed his yoke forward to dive the plane and get it as close to the ground as he dared. That way, only those enemy troops in its immediate vicinity could see it well enough to fire upon it.

Lero could not hear the screams of the passengers behind him. There was no time to comfort them. As he looked forward, he caught sight of two fighter jets coming directly toward him. He thought they would fire on him any second, but they streaked past him and passed out of his field of vision. Shortly, there was a large flash somewhere behind him outside of the plane. He concentrated on flying the plane. The fuel gauges indicated normal amounts, so if there were a hit on the tanks, the leakage was minimal. The controls responded to his inputs alright, and there was normal hydraulic pressure in the system.

For the first time, he keyed the mike to broadcast on the discrete frequency they had earlier decided on.

"Redbird is hit. Pilot and engineer killed. Substantial damage to flight deck. No fire. No leaks detected. Co-pilot flying with one arm. Shrapnel wound. Bleeding a lot. Need vector to nearest airport in Jordan."

There was a brief delay, then a woman's voice came over the frequency: "Redbird, roger. Fly heading one eight five. Border forty miles. Will advise airport later."

Lero keyed his mike, "Roger."

The terrain was rising and Redbird was now only about five hundred feet above the highest hills. Lero kept the power levers up to the stops. He knew at this altitude and power setting that the L-1011 was gulping fuel, but there was plenty. "Plus," he thought, "we only need about another ten minutes."

The plane was shaking. The shards of torn metal around the large hole that had been blasted in the left side of the flight deck moaned as the air streamed into and out of the hole. The gauges indicated that the number one engine on the left wing was overheating. If it were leaking oil, it would not last long.

"Come on, baby. Only a few more minutes," he spoke to no one as he stared into the black night ahead.

Chapter 68

Then, on the right just above him, a fighter jet appeared. Lero was tempted to take violent evasive maneuvers, but he spotted the blue star of David on the vertical stabilizer of the jet and knew instantly that it was Israeli.

'Redbird, fly heading of two one zero. Airport forty miles."

Jean could see the blip on her radar come to the new course, so she knew that the message was received.

"Please, God. Watch over them," she said to no one as she stared at the moving dot on the screen.

"Abraham, this is Naomi. Redbird is inbound for El Hussein airport. ETA eighteen minutes. Alert ground. Redbird damaged. Pilot and engineer probably dead. Co-pilot wounded and flying with one arm."

"Roger, Naomi," came the reply.

At El Hussein Airport, the claxon in the fire house blared to life. It was the middle of the night and bleary eyed fire fighters came awake. It seemed like chaos to the untrained observer, but every motion was rehearsed and pre-programmed. Within two minutes, Corporal

Miusci had the engine running in the foam truck and the other men were climbing aboard.

"Fire One manned and ready," he spoke into the handheld radio mike.

"Roger Fire One. Large passenger aircraft inbound, ETA ten minutes. Damaged by ground fire. Gear may not extend. Heavy with fuel. Large passenger manifest. Co-pilot flying with one arm."

"Roger," was all Miusci could muster.

All the firefighters in Fire One heard the transmission from ground control. By now, Fire two and three were alongside Fire one outside the fire house, idling, lights on.

"This could be a bad one," Miusci said to Hark, his right seat companion.

"Right," said Hark. "What else can we do?"

"Everybody got their fire suits on?" Miusci asked.

"Roger that," said Hark.

"He'll be here any time. ETA was ten minutes when we got the first call. I am going toward the runway and we will watch for him.

Miusci put the firetruck into gear and eased forward. The others followed suit. Since they did not know exactly where the jet would land or come to rest, they only went about half way from the firehouse to the runway and waited in the dark.

"Fire One, this is control. Foam the runway, beginning about a thousand feed down from the threshold."

"Roger, Fire One," said Miusci and put Fire One into gear. As soon as they reached the runway, he glanced at the pressure gauges and the auxiliary pump gauges. "Start the aux pump," he said to Hark, who instantly obeyed. As the truck accelerated down the runway, when they reached the second set of stripes, Hark opened the valves and Fire One began leaving a trail of foam about fifty feet wide. They sped on toward the far end of the runway.

As they got within five hundred feet of the far end, Hark said, "Chief, the foam is all used. What now?"

"I am going to stop near the end of the runway. Deploy two men to get into the ground level hatches and prep the fire hoses for use," said Miusci.

"Roger that," said Hark and turned to the fire suited men in the back seat. He pointed to two of them who nodded instantly.

Miusci brought the huge fire truck to a halt just fifty yards from the end of the runway. Firemen Murad and Howar leaped out and went to the metal hatch that was flush with ground level adjacent to the end of the side of the runway. The lifted the hatch doors and began pulling the fire hose out. Once it was out and lying beside the runway, they checked the pressure gauge. It read twenty pounds per square inch. They knew they were ready.

Chapter 69

"Redbird, you are clear of Syrian airspace. Fly heading two one five. Airport twenty two nautical. All lights on. Acknowledge," broadcast Jean from the Poseidon.

"Redbird roger. Looking."

Now that he was clear of Syrian airspace, Lero could turn on the running lights. He looked into the darkness for the runway lights ahead. He could still not move his left arm. Soon he would have to lean over and pull the thrust levers back with his right arm. He did his landing check list from memory. He pulled off some power and the huge airplane slowed. When it reached one hundred fifty knots, he pulled the gear lever down. From the way the plane wallowed, he could tell that the gear was coming down, but he got no indication from the lights on the panel that would indicate with three green lights that the gear was down and locked. There was no time to announce the approaching landing to the passengers. He hoped the commandos and other familiar people would warn the passengers to put on their seat belts and get ready for a rough landing.

"Redbird, field is twelve o'clock and eight miles."

"Redbird has the field."

"Good luck."

"Roger."

Lero leaned over and pulled the flap lever down to flaps ten. The big plane responded by slowing some more. He pulled off some thrust and they began to make their approach to the runway. He could see through the heavily damaged windscreen in front of him the lights of the runway and the flasher sequentially lighting the way to the runway threshold.

"Hang on, baby. Just a minute or so to the runway," he said to himself.

The spotter in a sedan near the threshold of runway two one called the tower. "Tower, Mobile five sees gear down on the approaching aircraft."

"Roger, Mobile Five. No way to tell them. Just good to know. Did you hear that Fire One?"

"Fire One, Roger. Here he comes."

By now, Lero had the L-1011 slowed to one hundred forty knots and had begun to bleed off some more power on his approach. Like he had done so many times as an airline pilot, he transitioned the big plane from slightly nose down to slightly nose up as they approached the runway. He noticed the airspeed bleeding off. Now one thirty. Then just as he saw the numbers at the threshold of the runway, he saw the airspeed settle on one twenty five. From here on, it was by feel. He raised the nose a little more and waited for the main gear to touch down. He knew that the main gear and the nose gear might collapse and he might be thrown to one side if one side collapsed and the other did not.

He saw the fire trucks waiting at the threshold and swept the big plane past them. He pulled back a bit on the yoke to raise the nose to slow the plane more and pulled the thrust levers all the way back.

He was beginning to see colored spots before his eyes as the main gear on both sides touched down. Things were getting blurry for him. He pulled the latches back on the three thrust levers to engage the thrust reversers. As the main gear touched down, he pushed the thrust levers with reversers engaged all the way forward and waited anxiously. The big plane did not yaw, indicating that there was no asymmetric force and all the thrust reversers were working. He had set the spoiler control in position as they swept down final and it now automatically deployed the spoilers on the tops of the wings, which contributed drag and spoiled lift, so the plane would not get airborne again if they bounced.

Just as things were settling down and his vision was becoming more blurred, the nose gear collapsed. The noise was indescribably loud. Sparks flew from the steel and aluminum metal that was now being shredded by the runway. The huge plane continued on, still decelerating, but it began to yaw to the right. Lero used the last of his consciousness to push the left rudder pedal to the stop and pull the thrust levers all the way back and hit the kill switch to cut off fuel to the engines and pulled the emergency brake handle. The yaw reduced a bit, but the big plane was clearly bound for the edge of the runway. Foam from the runway now intruded into the flight deck through the holes left by the missile and the damage being caused by the runway.

At this point, Lero lost consciousness. The plane was going about fifty miles an hour now and slowing rapidly. Fire Two was rapidly closing with the plane from behind and Miusci headed Fire One toward where he estimated the plane would stop from his position at the far end of the runway.

In its last two hundred yards of travel, the L-1011 left the runway to the right and plowed into the earth beside the runway. It came to a halt facing directly away from the runway. The commandos had the doors open before the plane stopped. Someone knew enough about L-1011s to set off the inflatable slides and as soon as the plane came to a halt, they triggered the inflators. There were steam and smoke and airborne fragments of runway foam in the air, but people began streaming down the slides. The rear slides were a little steeper than usual due to the fuselage angle because of the collapse of the nose gear. Trained firefighters trained their hoses on the passengers but did not turn on the water. Everyone hoped that there would be no fire, but all had that uppermost in their minds.

Two commandos kicked the partially open flight deck door and rushed in to help Lero. They could see that both Captain Rocco and the engineer were dead, so they concentrated on getting Lero loose from his belted position in the right seat. They gingerly, but gently, lifted him up and carried him with one man holding his legs and the other with both arms around his waist from behind. His left arm dangled and blood continued to run from his sleeve. They rushed him out and the one who had hold of his waist went down the chute with him. The firefighters at the foot of the chute grabbed Lero up and put him on a stretcher. One took out his scissors and deftly cut the front of Lero's shirt off. They instantly saw the bleeding gash at the top of his left arm and put a pressure dressing on it. Fireman Hinkle could see that there was no place to attach a tourniquet, so he held pressure on the wound and walked with the stretcher to the now waiting ambulance. The crowd of people parted to let them take Lero to the ambulance. They were strangely silent. As soon as the door shut and the fireman gave two slaps on the door, the ambulance accelerated away and turned on its flashers.

Chapter 70

"El Hussein tower, this is Naomi. Situation report, please."

"Naomi, this is El Hussein tower. L-1011 arrived. Nose gear collapsed on landing, Plane slewed off runway as it stopped. No fire. Repeat. No fire. Passengers evacuating at this time. Pilot and engineer dead. Co-pilot alive, but being transported to hospital. Lost a lot of blood. Only one casualty among passengers. Man hit in neck by ground fire, died immediately."

"Roger El Hussein tower. Thanks," said Naomi.

"Abraham, Abraham, this is Bluebird."

"Bluebird, this is Abraham. Go ahead."

"Bluebird is about fifty miles offshore over the Med, seventy nine nautical from the Incirlik VOR, requesting instructions and landing clearance."

"Bluebird, say fuel status."

"Bluebird has two hours fuel."

"Bluebird, stand by."

A minute later, Abraham control broadcast, "Blue Bird this is Abraham, fly heading one eight zero for vectors to Ovda. ETA thirty four minutes at present speed. Advise altitude."

"Roger, Abraham. Blue Bird is level at five hundred MSL and would like to climb to one zero, ten thousand feet."

"Roger, Blue Bird, climb to one zero, ten thousand feet approved, report reaching."

"Blue Bird roger."

Captain Honaker keyed the speaker system in the passenger compartment and said, "Ladies and gentlemen, those of you who understand English and speak Arabic relay this message to the others. We are clear of Syrian airspace and over the Mediterranean Sea about fifty miles offshore. We are going to an Israeli air base and expect to arrive there in approximately half an hour."

After a brief pause, there was a tremendous cheer from the passenger compartments. This flight meant many thing to many different groups, but they all recognized that they were free of the war zone and were going to a better situation.

Chapter 71

The phone beside the President's bed rang.

"Mr. President, sorry to wake you."

"It's alright, Mildred. What is up?"

"Just wanted you to know that both planes made it out of Syria alright. One crash landed at El Hussein airport in Jordan. One passenger killed by ground fire. Plane hit by missile. Nose gear collapsed on landing. Pilot and engineer dead. Co-pilot wounded by shrapnel in left shoulder, landed the plane with one arm. He lost a lot of blood and is in surgery now. Other plane is over the Mediterranean on its way to Ovda. No casualties, no damage."

"I see. Sounds like, even though there were some casualties, the mission went well, Mildred. Thanks."

"Thank you, Mr. President. Get some more sleep."

Chapter 72

Royal Jordanian army personnel surrounded the area where the plane came to rest and ushered the passengers and crew into the largest hangar on the base. Some of the children and older persons had difficulty walking on the uneven sandy soil, but the soldiers gave them plenty of time to walk. Inside the hangar, troops provided the refugees with food and drink. There were many smiling faces. Passengers congratulated each other at length.

After a bit, there was a bit of a stir at one end of the hangar. A man with a bullhorn addressed the crowd, first in English, then in Arabic. He said that His Majesty King Abdullah of Jordan would soon enter and would address the crowd. Everyone was elated, but respectfully quiet.

In a moment, several personal bodyguards in military uniforms entered and between them was King Abdullah. He took the bullhorn from the commandant and said, :"Ladies and gentlemen, welcome to the Kingdom of Jordan. You are free of Syria and its oppression. We will keep you here long enough to determine your best path to your next place of residence. There is plenty of food and drink. Mattresses and blankets will soon be provided to you.

For security reasons, none of you may leave until we ascertain your status and can notify relatives of your rescue. Military personnel among you will be called upon to identify yourselves and you will be repatriated to your country shortly, as soon as transportation can be arranged. I know all of you are tremendously grateful to the men who risked their lives to come to your rescue. A proper expression of gratitude will take place tomorrow. I should tell you that the other plane involved in your adventure was able to exit Syrian airspace without damage nor casualty and landed safely at an Israeli airbase. I regret to inform you that the Pilot Antonio Rocco and the engineer, Tucker Everson, on your plane were killed by the missile that damaged the plane. The copilot, identified to us only as "Lero," suffered a serious shoulder wound from the missile and landed the plane with one arm. He is now in surgery at one of our hospitals, receiving the best medical care available. Those of you who have loved ones or family or unit members on the other plane will be joined with them in short order. I have taken the liberty to personally talk with the President of the United States who planned and orchestrated this operation and have congratulated him and his many associates who worked together to organize this rescue. Now get some rest, congratulate each other and say a prayer of thanksgiving for your rescue and for the souls of the deceased pilot and flight engineer. Welcome to the Kingdom of Jordan."

Chapter 73

"South Med Approach, Navy four five two six six."

"Four five two six six, this is Med Approach, go ahead."

Approach, four five two six six is one hundred five DME east of Aviano, level at Flight Level two four zero, requesting landing instructions."

"Four five two six six, we show you one hundred DME east of Aviano now. Your IFF shows two four zero. Squawk four zero three five for us please. Fly heading two six five and begin your descent to six thousand feet."

"Roger, four five two six six out of two four zero for six, squawking four zero three five."

When the Poseidon taxied in, it had been airborne for fourteen hours and five minutes. The crew was weary and walked slowly, carrying their baggage. A solitary figure in civilian clothes waited at the front of the hangar near where they came to a halt. As Jean approached, he stepped forward.

"Jefe," she said, as she wrapped her arms around his neck. "So good of you to come. What is the word? I know he is in the hospital, in surgery."

As he held her with his arms around her waist, she shook with sobs.

"They had to graft an artery in his left shoulder. It is touch and go for now. If the graft fails, he may lose the arm. He is lucky to be alive. He flew the plane the last hundred miles with one arm. He has lost a lot of blood. You need to rest tonight and we will fly over to be with him tomorrow."

"Thank you, Harry," she sobbed. He gathered up her bag and helped her to the car.

Chapter 74

The phone rang in the quarters of the Chief of Staff.

"Chief of Staff's quarters, Sergeant Mikel speaking."

"Sergeant Mikel, inform the Chief of Staff that both planes have landed. One at Ovda and the other at El Hussein Airport in Jordan. One casualty, a civilian on the plane that landed in Jordan. Pilot and Engineer killed, co-pilot injured and in surgery. Tell the Chief that his grandson and his unit are safe in Jordan."

"Will do. Thanks."

General Haim had heard the telephone ring in the parlor. He came from the bedroom, tying the sash of his robe.

"What is it, sergeant?"

"First of all, your grandson is safe in Jordan," said Mikel, then relayed the remainder of the message he had just received.

General Haim nodded and smiled and returned to his bedroom. The sergeant could see through the crack in the door, the General kneeling beside the bed and sobbing.

Chapter 75

Winston Churchill once said that the most exhilarating feeling on earth is to be shot at and realize that the shot had missed.

Jean cracked the door open to the room. Lero was awake and looking at the door. She swept in and went to him. He reached up to hug her with his right arm. They hugged for a long time. One more time, Lero had risked his life for others and survived. They both knew the significance of this meeting.

It was late in the afternoon. She had flown with Jefe from Aviano and she was exhausted from her flight on the Poseidon and from worrying about him. The nurse came in about half an hour later and found them both on the bed, sound asleep. His good arm was around her waist.

Epilogue

Seven months later.

Jean was at the front desk when the phone rang. She recognized the voice immediately.

"Jean, this is Mr. Murfree. May I speak to Lero, please?

"Oh, yes sir. Just a moment."

She buzzed Lero in the back office on the intercom.

"Mr. Murfree calling," she said.

"Thanks," he said.

"Hello."

"Say the word, please,"

"Houston. Say the word."

"Santa Fe."

Now they both knew with whom they were speaking.

"How are you doing?" asked the President.

"Good, sir. My shoulder is healing nicely. I don't have full mobility yet, but my strength is returning thanks to Jean's good care."

"Do you and she feel well enough to join Janice and me for dinner in Phoenix next Thursday?"

"Certainly. Thank you. Where?"

"We are staying at the Hyatt Regency. Security will be tight. You will be asked for a password before you can access our floor. The word is 'Rodeo.'"

"Fine, sir. What time?"

"Let's say seven. I will let you know any changes."

"Sounds great. See you then."

"Okay. Thanks," said the President, and he rang off.

When Lero told Jean, she smiled a knowing smile and said, teasingly, "Well, I will just have to have a new outfit if we are going to dinner with the President and the First Lady."

Lero smiled and nodded.

The next day, instead of going to Sonic for lunch, Lero drove her to downtown Tucson to the nicest store in town to buy her the outfit she wanted. He told the saleslady that she could have anything she wanted, but he knew that Jean would be reasonable, as always. He retreated to a discreet distance and let her and sales lady have a thorough encounter.

Jean picked a dignified dark blue pants suit and a frilly white blouse. The sales lady suggested a matching pair of pumps and said that if the event was that important, she should pick out some appropriate undergarments and hose.

When she nodded and waved, he came back over and paid the saleslady. She hugged his arm as he handed his charge card over.

"That was so sweet of you," she said as she held onto him tight enough that their hips bounced against the other as they walked.

"Jean, I owe you so much for nursing me back to good health. I love you so much. This is just a small token of my gratitude."

They had put the office phone on forward to his cell phone and locked the place up before they drove to lunch.

They went back to the home they shared and got ready for the trip to Phoenix, about an hour and a half away.

The Grand Cherokee ate up the ninety miles in the late afternoon sunlight. The desert highway shimmered in the heat. Lero kept the headlights on as they drove so any oncoming car could see them through the waves of heat.

As they pulled up to the Hyatt Regency, at the entry, a gentleman in a blue blazer and khaki pants stepped up to their car as Lero stopped. Lero rolled the window down and the man gestured that he wanted to speak to Lero.

"Sir, I am Secret Service. If you will leave the motor running, we will secure your car. It will be here for you when you come back out."

"Thank you very much, sir," said Lero and opened the door. He went around and helped Jean out and they walked arm in arm into the polished brass doorway.

As they stepped up to the elevators, the Secret Service agent there said to them, "Floor twenty one, sir."

"Thanks," said Lero and pushed the button for 'Up.'

When they exited the elevator on the twenty first floor, they were directed by the Secret Service agents there to walk through the metal detector, which they did.

"It's the third door on the right, sir," said the agent to them as they cleared the metal detector.

As they approached the door, it opened and the President and First Lady stepped out to greet them. It was an emotional event for all four of them. Sending your friends into harm's way is very difficult for sensitive people and President Thompson and Janice had prayed for the safety of Lero and Jean and all the men and women involved in the operation. There was a lot of release in the reunion on the twenty first floor.

As they sat down to dinner, President Thompson said, "Before we eat, let me say a blessing. 'Dear Lord, thank you for this meal which we are about to enjoy according to your bounty. Please bless the souls of those lost in the recent rescue mission in Syria. Comfort those who lost loved ones in the mission. Thank you for the valiant efforts of all of those involved in rescuing refugees, friendly military personnel, those secretly working behind enemy lines, and friendly diplomatic personnel from the war torn area. We are especially grateful for our friends here with us tonight, for their devotion to duty and their sacrifice. Please bless this meal to the use of our bodies and bless us to your continued service, in Jesus' name we pray. Amen.'"

There was a considerable pause before anyone spoke. There were sniffles and stifled sobs.

The stewards waiting to serve the salads had to pause for a while before serving the salads. No one spoke as they all tried to gather themselves back from a very emotional moment. Feelings swept over them all, for separate and different reasons. They all had to deal with that and they chose to do so in silence.

Finally, in order to signal to the servers that they were ready to be served, the President looked over to them and nodded soberly. As the servers set the salads in front of the four diners, the mood turned more relieved and they all sensed a return to the present tense with some relief.

Rather than speak, each of them began eating the salad. It was a while before anyone spoke.

First Lady Janice Thompson was the first to speak.

"It is impossible to put into words how grateful we are to you both. We both prayed incessantly for you and the others while the operation was under way. We told no one on the White House staff about the operation and they probably wondered why we seemed preoccupied at times. Fred and I feel so close to you both and we are so glad to be with you again."

Jean said, "Thank you so much for all you have done for us and our team. We are so grateful for the opportunity to serve. Our people are dedicated and motivated, largely because of the leadership and inspiration you both have given us."

Finally, Lero spoke, "Mr. President, Fred, it is very difficult to put into words how grateful we are for your trust and support, for the way you have watched over us as we have worked for our country. Our people are very grateful. We feel your support each day as we go about our tasks."

He paused to gather his feelings before he spoke again.

"I am especially grateful for the medical care you helped coordinate after my injury on this latest mission. We felt your and Janice's care and concern constantly. Thank you."

There was another long pause before anyone spoke.

The President, uncharacteristically at a loss for words, hesitated, then said "Clearly, there is nothing we can do, of a material nature, to adequately demonstrate to you our appreciation for your leadership, from both of you, and for your zealous execution of the suggested tasks we have put before you.

However, as a small token of our appreciation, and that of the whole country, if they knew what you have done, we have arranged to pay off the existing mortgage balance on Jean's home in Tucson, and we have placed a token of appreciation in a savings account in your joint names at your bank.

In order to dispel some concerns you may have about providing for your continued financial security in retirement, we have purchased a joint and survivor annuity in both of your names that should make you comfortable in the future."

Lero and Jean were stunned by the generosity.

Everyone at the table sensed that all were having a difficult time with their emotions. There was a long silence. The servers paused, rather than retrieve the salad dishes, and waited for a more appropriate moment to do so.

Lero choked a bit, then said "Thank you very much, Mr. President. That is very generous. But, do you want me and Jean to retire?"

"No, Dan. You and Jean are much too precious to us and our country for that. I just want you to be more careful to keep yourself from having to put yourself into harm's way in the future. We hope to enjoy our retirement having you and Jean as close friends."

Then, to break the mood into a more jovial direction the President asked, "Will you share an O'Douls with me? The ladies are having a California Merlot."

(Neither the President nor Lero drink alcohol. O'Doul's is a non-alcoholic beer that they both favor)

The servers removed the salad plates and served the broiled Pacific Salmon. Dinner took on a much more celebratory tone.

As the servers put the dessert on table, Janice spoke.

"It is going to be late for you both to drive back across the desert to Tucson. Please stay here tonight and have an early breakfast with us tomorrow. Fred is speaking to the American Manufacturers Association national convention at noon and we will fly back to Washington after that. There is a spare room down the hall."

Jean spoke for herself and Lero. "That is so kind of you. Of course, we will stay."

By the time they finished the frozen yogurt and fresh strawberries, it was almost ten. All four of them had had a long day. They said a friendly 'good evening' and Lero and Jean walked down the hall to their waiting room. A steward handed them room keys and opened the door for them.

Lero asked if it would be more convenient for him to retrieve their overnight bag from the car or have someone bring it. The steward replied that it would be brought up right away.

In the morning, after a great breakfast with their friends. Lero and Jean went out to the Grand Cherokee and pointed it south toward Tucson.